"I'd pay a pe___ ___ ___ ___ ___. A ___ and now-familiar ma_____ voice interrupted Sinclair's thoughts. "In fact, I'd pay a whole dollar to find out what's putting that frown on your pretty face."

Ben eased into the vacant seat next to her. Suddenly, the temperature in the Crystal Room got a lot hotter.

"I'm not frowning," Sinclair replied, all too aware of just how close to her Ben was sitting. His knees touched hers, and that simple touch sent vibrations of pleasure throughout her body. She still didn't understand the effect that Ben Easington had on her. True, it had been a while since she'd been intimate with a man, but this wild urge to explore every part of his body with her lips was perplexing. She'd never thought of herself as a passionate woman, but her hands longed to run themselves all over his bare skin, like a sex-starved wanton.

Ben leaned closer and whispered, "You're making me blush. You're undressing me with your eyes."

Sinclair felt the blood drain from her face. Oh my God, he was a damn mind reader! How could he know what she was thinking about doing with him, and to him? She felt the frown that she'd denied having grow deeper.

He flashed her a wide smile. "I'm kidding, Sinclair! It's just wishful thinking on my part."

PET DIVA
FINDS LOVE

Janette McCarthy

Kensington Publishing Corp.

http://www.kensingtonbooks.com

DAFINA BOOKS are published by

Kensington Publishing Corp.
850 Third Avenue
New York, NY 10022

All Kensington Titles, Imprints, and Distributed Lines are available at special quantity discounts for bulk purchases for sales promotions, premiums, fund-raising, and educational or institutional use. Special book excerpts or customized printings can also be created to fit specific needs. For details, write or phone the office of the Kensington special sales manager: Kensington Publishing Corp., 850 Third Avenue, New York, NY 10022, attn: Special Sales Department, Phone: 1-800-221-2647.

Dafina and the Dafina logo Reg. U.S. Pat. & TM Off.

ISBN:13: 978-0-7582-1582-6
ISBN:10: 0-7582-1582-7

First mass market printing: December 2007

10 9 8 7 6 5 4 3 2 1

Printed in the United States of America

*This novel is dedicated to
my beloved soul sister
Dr. Angelita Covington Reed*

Acknowledgments

First and foremost, to God be all the glory! Everything I have accomplished in this life has been a direct result of His blessings! I would like to thank the men in my life, Jamaal, Mark & Paul, for their love, support, and continual good humor, especially where I am concerned. To my mother, Brenda, the original diva, thanks for providing me with continual inspiration. Your advice to always put God first has been the guiding force in my life. Thanks to my little nieces, Khadijah and Khalilah, for bringing me joy, light, and laughter every day. And to Barbara, representing for St. Lucia. Keep holding it down, girlfriend! You are truly my sister! There aren't enough words to thank my girls. You know you keep a sister on the straight and narrow. Thanks to Stephanie, Kathi Vonda, Lessie, Robyn, Lonya, Joyce, Nancy, Charmaine, Diane, Joy, Latisha, and Lynne for always being there—strong, loyal and true. I hope that all of you know how much I love you and how thankful I am that you are in my life! To my C-town crew—Teri, Betsy, Leah, Lisa, Meredith, Faith (my favorite Yardie!), Linda, Caprice, Valerie, Karla, Carolyn, and Kiki—thanks for being there through it all! To my roomie, Sarah. After all these years, our bond is as strong as ever! To my soul brother Marlon P., thanks for being such a wonderful friend, and thanks for sharing Kathi with me! To Marla and Frank, thanks for not forgetting me and always making me feel welcome despite the vicissitudes of life. This means more to me than I can say. To my Jamaican crew, big ups! To my wonderful editor, Rakia Clark, who is as patient as she is kind! I look forward to making more beautiful music together. To my agent, Manie Barron. Thanks, Boo! To anyone who has ever supported my work, I say thank you from the bottom of my heart! Finally, as always, to Dr. Voldie Osmond McCarthy, my dearly beloved father. I miss you every single day, but just like you told me, Daddy, true love lives on forever! Thank you for always believing in my dreams, no matter how crazy they were. Thank you for showing me what a strong, wonderful, loving man looks like. Love you!

Prologue

The Unfaithful Dog

"Hi. This is Sinclair, the Pet Diva, and you're on the air. Tell me what's going on with the animal in your life."

Sinclair Dearheart adjusted the microphone in the small studio and tried to get more comfortable in her chair. Radio WILD was a struggling AM radio station with a small but loyal audience. It was also the home of *The Pet Diva Show*, a weekly call-in talk show featuring Sinclair's alter ego, the Pet Diva, in which pet owners called in for advice on various issues affecting their beloved pets. Sinclair fielded the nonmedical-issue questions, and her best friend and on-air assistant, Melody, a trained veterinarian, dealt with any medical issues. Since its inception, seven months ago, *The Pet Diva Show* had been one of the station's most successful programs. Sinclair often worried that the day might come when there would be nothing fresh or original to say about pets, their owners, and the various issues facing both the pets and the folks that loved, spoiled, and doted on them. So far, that day hadn't come.

The caller's strident voice filled the small studio. It was a woman—a woman who was obviously fed up. "I'm tired, sick and tired, of that unfaithful dog."

Sinclair had heard and seen a lot in the thirty years that she'd been living, but she'd never heard of an unfaithful dog—a disloyal cat maybe, a temperamental dog perhaps, but never an unfaithful dog. In fact, it had been her experience that dogs were among the most faithful and loyal of God's creations.

She took a quick sip of water before responding to the caller. "Maybe something's going on with your pet," Sinclair replied. "Dogs aren't usually known to be . . . um, unfaithful."

Sinclair wondered briefly at the choice of the word *unfaithful*. Once again, that wasn't a word that was often used in relation to a pet. It was, however, a word that she was all too familiar with. It was a word that applied to her ex-husband, Wayne, a word that she had used to explain to him the reason she'd filed for divorce. It was a word that even now, three years after her divorce, still caused pain.

"Mine is," the caller shot back. "He's been unfaithful since the day I brought him home."

Melody joined in the conversation. "Who's your dog been cheating with?"

Sinclair shot Melody the same look she gave her in fifth grade, right after Melody started a fistfight with the school bully. Melody had ignored her then, just as she ignored her now. Just like in fifth grade, Melody did exactly what she wanted to do and dealt with the consequences later.

"Who *hasn't* he been sleeping with is a better question!" the caller snapped, her indignation growing as she continued speaking. "He's . . . he's . . . well, he's indiscriminate!"

Indiscriminate? Also an interesting choice of words to use about her pet. Sinclair began to wonder if this was yet another crazy caller. Last month they'd had two callers who fell under that category: one thought his pet poodle Michael Jackson was possessed by the spirit of the devil, and the other was upset that her Pomeranian kept staring at her, especially when she was naked.

Sinclair decided it was time to jump into the conversation, before Melody lost her patience completely. Melody didn't suffer fools lightly; nor did she have much patience with the insane. Although Sinclair couldn't classify the caller as insane, there was clearly something *off* about her.

"Have you tried getting him fixed?" asked Sinclair.

"Fixed!" the caller snorted. "Like that would do any good. But I guess he can't help it . . . He's a dog."

This time Melody couldn't help herself. "Dogs are loyal by nature. Are you sure there isn't something you're doing that's causing this problem?"

Sinclair shook her head. Insulting the callers was not exactly the best way to grow their radio audience.

"I've been good to him. There's nothing I did to make him want to go and sleep with my best friend," replied the caller.

This comment was met with a stunned silence. Mike, the producer of the show, held up a handwritten sign that read COMMERCIAL BREAK. But Sinclair had to continue the conversation. After all, this was a family show. Some points had to be clarified.

"Tell me that your best friend is a dog," said Sinclair.

"She is now," said the caller. "For her to sleep with my man is just *low-down!*"

"Your man?" Melody asked. "Okay, now we're confused. Are you talking about a man or a dog?"

Mike waved the COMMERCIAL BREAK sign in the air like a flag.

The caller sighed. "I'm talking about a man who acts like a dog. I'm talking about my boyfriend."

Sinclair stifled the giggles that rose in her throat, while Melody wasn't as successful, as a fit of laughter overcame her.

Clearing her throat, Sinclair said in her serious, radio personality voice, "Ma'am, are you aware that this is a show about pets and their issues?"

"I know what this show is about!" the caller responded. "I listen every week. I'm a pet lover. Got two cats and a parakeet. We all love your show!"

Sinclair cleared her throat again. "Thank you. But, ma'am, if you know that this is a pet show, why are you calling in about your boyfriend?"

"Ex-boyfriend!" said the caller. "I've kicked that bum to the curb. I'm just sick and tired of his cheating."

Melody's laughter subsided enough for her to ask, "What does your boyfriend's cheating have to do with a show about pet issues?"

The caller thought about it for a moment. Then she replied, "I guess I figured that Cedric . . . that's his name . . . is an animal, and this is a show about animals and their behavior. I thought maybe y'all could shed some light on this issue . . . maybe give me some advice."

Sinclair could shed a little light, but not from the perspective of a professional who'd dealt with animals for several years, but as someone who'd loved a cheater. "My advice is to move on."

Melody reached over and squeezed Sinclair's hand. After the divorce, Sinclair's life had fallen quietly, but still dramatically, apart. She hadn't had a nervous breakdown, but she'd come close. She'd lost interest in almost everything that had given her joy as she'd watched the man she'd once loved publicly humiliate her by parading his latest conquest around town and, worse, turn into a monster, who demanded that she compensate him financially for the three years they'd been married.

Melody had been there in court when the man Sinclair had put through law school yelled at her that she'd never done anything for him. She'd been there for Sinclair when he moved out of their home on their wedding anniversary. Melody had been there when folks who had nothing better to do had spread news about Sinclair's ex and all the wonderful things he was doing with yet another woman. Melody had been there during the bad times, and she knew how much effort it had taken for Sinclair to fight her way back and reclaim her life.

Sinclair smiled at her friend. Things were better now. She could look at her ex-husband without experiencing the searing pain that came from a broken heart. She was better now—not great, but better.

Sinclair leaned closer to the microphone. She wanted Cedric, and every other cheating man, to hear her words. "And if you're out there listening, Cedric, you're a fool. What goes around comes around."

"Next caller," said Melody quickly.

"You're on the air with Sinclair, the Pet Diva. Tell me what's going on with the animal in your life."

A man's voice filled the studio. "Sinclair, this is Cedric . . . the guy you and my ex were just talking about. I'm a big fan of the show . . . I used to listen with my ex. . . ."

Sinclair braced herself for an angry response from the cheating Cedric. "What can I do for you, Cedric?"

"You can go out on a date with me," replied Cedric. "Are you as sexy as you sound?"

Sinclair hit the button that disconnects callers quickly. Speaking into the microphone, she purred, "Sorry, Cedric. One cheater in a lifetime is more than enough. And one more thing. All you listeners out there, stop calling cheating men dogs . . . Dogs are loyal. Dogs love you unconditionally. They don't care if you're fat, thin, tall, short, beautiful, or have a face that only a blind mother could love. They will never desert you. So go ahead and call cheating men every terrible name in the book, but just don't call them dogs! This is Sinclair, the Pet Diva, and we're overdue for a commercial break!"

"So," Melody chimed in, in an obvious attempt to change the subject, "how are your sister's wedding plans going?"

Sinclair shook her head. Her sister, Roxie, had been planning this wedding for months, and now that the day was finally near, Roxie's usually calm nerves had disappeared, along with her good sense of humor.

"Another sore subject?" asked Melody.

"No," Sinclair replied. "I'm a little worried about Roxie."

"What's going on?"

"I'm not sure," Sinclair replied. "She just seems really nervous."

"Well, she is getting married in two weeks. Most brides-to-be get a little nervous at this point."

Sinclair remembered her own experience as a bride-to-be and felt that familiar dull pain that accompanied all memories of her marriage. She'd been divorced three years now—enough time not to still feel the sense of loss and sadness that accompanied the demise of her marriage. She'd been a ridiculously happy bride on her way to marry the man of her dreams. A few months later she'd realized that she'd made a mistake: her husband hadn't shared the same vision of forsaking all others until death do them part. She'd waited three years, hoping he'd change, that he'd one day wake up and do right, until one day she realized that he'd never do right by her.

The bright red ON AIR sign flashed in the small studio, and Sinclair pushed all thoughts of her marriage away.

"This is Sinclair, the Pet Diva. Talk to me."

A familiar male voice filled the studio.

"It's me, Sinclair." Cedric had called again. "Can I have a date?"

Chapter 1

Sinclair slipped out of the wedding rehearsal dinner at her mother's country club and headed to the outside patio. She needed to get some air. She needed to breathe. *Okay,* she reasoned, *pull yourself together. This is a wedding, not a funeral.* For Sinclair, those two subjects brought out very similar emotions, and that was the problem. She was happy for her sister, Roxie. Roxie had meticulously planned her wedding from her sixth birthday. In fact, she'd planned everything down to the one remaining detail—the identity of the groom. The groom had made himself apparent six months ago in the person of Everett Iverson, a gorgeous, sincere, successful attorney, who was devoted to Roxie. They'd gotten engaged in Paris three months later, and now they were about to become man and wife. Sinclair was happy for her sister. Everett was going to be a wonderful husband. They were destined to live a happily ever after life, but right at that very moment, Sinclair just needed to breathe.

From the patio, Sinclair could hear the sound of

conversation and general merriment. The soft
music from the jazz trio her future brother-in-law
had hired soothed her. The wedding rehearsal
dinner was a success. Her mother would be very,
very happy. The dinner was being held in one of
the private reception rooms—the same reception
room that she'd had her own rehearsal dinner in
six years ago. Although tradition dictated that the
groom was responsible for the wedding rehearsal
dinner, Roxie had chosen the venue. "Is it going to
be a problem if we have the dinner at Mom's
club?" Roxie had asked her, and Sinclair had assured her sister that it was fine. No problems here.
The way Sinclair reasoned, it was Roxie's wedding,
and as her sister, Sinclair wasn't about to rain on
that particular parade. She took off her high-heel
sandals—they were killing her feet—and stood
barefoot on the patio.

She'd thought she could handle it. But sitting in
the same room where she'd had so much hope
years before had brought a surprising lump to her
throat. *Damn. Damn. Damn.* She needed to get past
this. Years of therapy, long conversations with supportive and outraged girlfriends, and countless self-
help books had helped, but it was apparent that she
hadn't completely gotten over her divorce. Although she no longer loved her ex-husband, the
hurt she'd felt over his betrayal hadn't vanished. It
didn't help that her mother, Belinda Rose, who
lived in eternal hope that she'd reconcile with her
ex, had invited him to the wedding.

Sinclair and her sister had both been vehemently
opposed to inviting Wayne Celestin to the wedding,
but their mother was an immovable force when she

made her mind up, and she was bound and determined to include her ex-son-in-law in Roxie's big day. Wayne's mother, Rosemarie, remained one of Belinda Rose's best friends, despite their offsprings' less-than-amicable divorce. "I won't snub Rosemarie or her son," Belinda Rose had declared. "Besides," her mother had declared to Sinclair, "if I can face your father, then you certainly can face Wayne."

Her mother had a point there. If Sinclair's divorce could be described as hostile, her parents' divorce was nothing short of a nuclear meltdown. They hadn't spoken to each other in years, and her mother still referred to her father as "that despicable man I should never have married." Belinda Rose would manage to deal with her bad feelings about the father of her children long enough to get through the wedding of her youngest daughter.

Having her father come to the wedding was a joy for Sinclair. After her parents' divorce, he'd moved back to his native Jamaica, and she'd only seen him once or twice a year after that. Despite the time and the distance, Sinclair's love for her father was unequivocal and unwavering. The divorce of her parents should have been a clue to her that sometimes happily ever after doesn't show up. Sometimes it gets waylaid. Still, Sinclair had remained optimistic that she was going to find the love she read about in her secret stash of romance novels, where the hero and the heroine always ended up together. Even now, after Wayne broke her heart, she harbored a secret, although somewhat distant, hope that the man whom God had intended for her would show up. She wasn't exactly holding her breath, though.

The warm August night held a sense of promise.

There was something about an ink-black sky exploding with stars that caused her spirits to rise. A light breeze caressed her skin, and she closed her eyes for a moment, trying to savor this rare moment of calm. The past week had been crazy, with last-minute dress fittings, bride-to-be hysteria, general drama from her mother—although that couldn't be attributed to the wedding; her mother was born with drama stamped on her forehead—and a feeling of dread, a feeling that despite all the merriment, something wasn't quite right.

Sinclair couldn't quite figure out what it was that was causing this bad feeling. True, after her divorce, she'd avoided weddings like a vampire avoids sunlight, but she'd managed to put her aversion to weddings firmly in check. This was Roxie's big day, and Sinclair was going to do everything in her power to concentrate on helping make this day as happy and wonderful as Roxie had dreamt it would be. But there was something that wasn't quite right. Maybe it was just the nervousness that came from the prospect of seeing Wayne again. She hadn't seen him in over a year, and she wasn't looking forward to seeing him again.

The last time she'd seen him, he was with yet another beautiful woman, dining at a restaurant she'd gone to with Roxie and Melody. She'd managed to get through the meal, but the unabashed adoration with which Wayne had stared at his date had caused Sinclair to lose her appetite—even though she'd been at one of her favorite restaurants in New York City. Wayne had never stared at her like that. She wondered if he was bringing the woman to the wedding, but she couldn't bring herself to ask her mother or Roxie. *Besides,* she reasoned, *what difference does it make at this point?* They'd been divorced for three years. It was obvious that Wayne had moved on. Hell, it was his moving on that had caused her to file for divorce in the first place.

She'd moved on also. She'd had a few relationships, but nothing serious, and nothing that caused her heart to race the way it did when she first met Wayne. She was currently flying solo, and for the first time in her life, that was just fine with her. She didn't want to be in a relationship right now. She was busy with her practice and her radio show. Whenever she needed romance, she could pick up a novel or watch her favorite DVDs. As for companionship, her Yorkshire terrier, Princess, gave her all the companionship she needed. She certainly didn't yearn for or need a man. She took another deep breath and let the warm August breeze continue its caress.

Sinclair hadn't meant to scream. But the sudden touch of a hand on her bare arm both startled and frightened her. She turned to find herself facing a man who could only be described as being nothing short of beautiful. He was tall. At six feet, Sinclair was used to being eye-to-eye with most men, but she had to look up to see his face. He was dark-skinned, with large, piercing brown eyes. He had an exotic air about him, with his full lips; high cheekbones; and long, dark eyebrows, which were now slightly raised as he regarded her with an expression somewhere between bewilderment and amusement. Sinclair couldn't tell. His hair was cut close to his scalp, and he had a small gold earring in his right ear.

But it was his mouth that got Sinclair's full attention. There was something about those full lips, the slight upward tilt, as if there were a smile on its way, that caused her breath to catch in her throat. She fought the urge to kiss those lips. What on earth was wrong with her? Sinclair hadn't felt an instant attraction to a man in years, and she'd begun to wonder if she could ever feel that way again. Staring at this man's seductive mouth elicited an immediate and very strong reaction. She felt something she hadn't felt in a long time. She felt passion. She felt heat.

"I didn't mean to startle you," he said, even as he flashed a smile at her, which immediately caused Sinclair to think inappropriate and indecent thoughts.

If his mouth awakened her long-dormant passion, the combination of a rich, deep voice and a Southern accent sealed the deal. This man was sex appeal personified.

Sinclair cleared her throat. Tearing her gaze away from his mesmerizing mouth to focus on his dark eyes, she said. "Are you looking for someone?"

The sexy mouth curved into a smile. "As a matter of fact, I am," he replied. "I'm looking for you."

Ben Easington was used to seeing beautiful women. He'd traveled all over the world in his career as a freelance sports journalist, and his journeys had brought him in contact with beautiful women of all sorts of colors, shapes, and sizes. His ex had been an extremely beautiful woman. He appreciated beauty as much as the next man. Hell, maybe more. But he'd never had the kind of reaction to a woman, to any woman, that he had when he'd entered the patio and found the delectable Sinclair Dearheart standing there, eyes closed, head tilted back—with that slinky gold dress blowing in the breeze. Her shoulder-length hair was worn in loose curls that danced in the breeze. Her long brown legs were bare, and the red nail polish on her toes all but did him in. The fact that she was barefoot was an added bonus. He felt as if someone had slammed something in his gut. Hard.

For the last six months, he'd heard just about all he could stomach on the subject of Sinclair Dearheart. His best friend, Everett, was marrying Sinclair's sister, and almost from the time Everett fell in love with Roxie, he'd been determined to set Ben up on a date with Sinclair. From everything Ben had heard about Sinclair, she appeared to be some kind of nut. A pet psychiatrist? What the hell was that? From everything he'd heard, he imagined some Doctor Dolittle freak who believed that animals were talking to her. He'd done his best to avoid meeting Sinclair. His life was complicated enough without adding into the mix a woman whose elevator, he was convinced, didn't go to the top floor. He'd come to the wedding rehearsal dinner late. His flight from Brazil had been delayed by several hours. He'd just had time to rush home, take a hot shower, and change, and still, he was two hours late for the rehearsal dinner. He'd completely missed the wedding rehearsal. As soon as he'd gotten to the dinner, Everett had sent him on a mission to find his missing future sister-in-law. When he stepped out on the patio, he was surprised by what he found. He hadn't expected to find one of the sexiest women he'd seen in a long time. He hadn't expected the immediate need to take her into his arms and kiss her senseless. He hadn't expected this.

"You're looking for me?" Her voice was low and husky. He'd heard that she was also a radio disk jockey. With a voice like that, he could see why. He felt his insides tighten. Damn, he really wanted to kiss her.

He regained his composure. "Everett sent me to get you. They're about to start dinner."

Ben sensed their close physical proximity disturbed her, despite her placid demeanor. She had to feel the same heat that he felt.

"Well, thank you," she said, dismissing him, with a cool smile. "I'll be right in."

Ben wasn't ready to be dismissed.

He took a step closer. "I'm Ben. Ben Easington."

Her eyes widened in recognition. "Everett's friend?"

"The one and only."

They were close enough for him to pull her firmly in his arms. She smelled like vanilla. He watched as her gold hoop earrings dangled in the breeze and he felt an almost irresistible pull of attraction.

"I've heard a lot about you," she said, with a smile.

He felt inordinately pleased. "Have you?"

"Yes, indeed."

Ben felt his control start to slip away. The combination of warm summer breezes, the scent of vanilla, and the most beautiful woman he'd seen in a good long time was weakening whatever self-control he thought he possessed. He had to taste those lips. He wanted to feel her in his arms. He wanted to stroke those long brown arms. He wanted to take her right there on the patio and make wild love to her. He wanted to hear that sultry voice tell him exactly what she wanted him to do to her.

"What have you heard?" he asked, trying to keep his wits about him.

"Well, it depends on the source," Sinclair replied, taking a step back from him and widening the space between them. She felt the same attraction. He knew it. It made her uncomfortable. This was going to be a very interesting evening. "I've heard that you're an unapologetic womanizer, and I've heard that you're a saint."

"I'd say that both of those descriptions are inaccurate," Ben replied as he stepped toward her, closing the gap between them. *Checkmate.* He watched as she bit her bottom lip. She was nervous. *Good.*

Sinclair cleared her throat. "We really should be getting inside."

Ben didn't move. "We really should."

For one crazy moment, he debated taking her in his arms, right there and then. But he knew he'd scare her away. He'd have to be patient with Sinclair Dearheart. He wanted her; they both knew it. But he'd wait until the time was right.

Ben took a step back. "I'll see you inside, Sinclair."

* * *

Sinclair bent down to put on her sandals. She didn't want to go inside yet, but she knew she couldn't hide out on the patio forever, especially since her future brother-in-law had already dispatched someone to summon her. But just as she was about to go inside, her sister Roxie stepped out on the patio.

"Mind if I join you?" Roxie walked over to her sister. "I'd like to hide out, too."

Sinclair adjusted the straps on her sandals and then stood to face her sister.

"Brides aren't supposed to hide," Sinclair replied. "Especially brides as pretty as you."

Roxie was a beautiful woman. She looked more like their father's side of the family, with her copper-colored skin and light brown hair. Unlike Sinclair, who was tall and slender, Roxie was shorter, with more womanly curves. She had a small waist, with full hips, and men regularly fell madly in love with her. It was not surprising that Everett was besotted with his future wife. Roxie had her father's green eyes, and right now those green eyes looked troubled.

"What's wrong?" Sinclair asked.

"Nothing," Roxie replied. "Everything."

"That doesn't make sense, Sis."

Sinclair watched as Roxie took a deep breath. "I'm scared, Sinclair. What if I'm making a mistake? Look what happened to you and Mom."

Sinclair felt a slice of pain that should have been dulled by now. Being known as a veteran of divorce wars was not a pleasant thing.

"Mom and I married the wrong men," Sinclair replied.

"Yeah, but how do you know who the wrong man is? I know that when you got married, you never thought you'd ever divorce."

Sinclair nodded her head. "That's true. But in my case and in Mom's case, there were signs. Wayne cheated on me when we were dating, and I still married him, and as for Mom, she knew that Daddy was already married to his work when she met him. Everett is perfect for you. He loves you, and he's a good man."

Roxie started to cry. "He is a good man," she whispered.

Sinclair walked over and hugged her sister. "Everything is going to work out," she said. "You're just having pre-wedding jitters."

Roxie pulled away from her sister's embrace and wiped her eyes. She placed a wavering smile on her lips and said, "I'm sure you're right. I'm sorry that Mom invited Wayne to the wedding. I tried to stop her."

Sinclair shrugged her shoulders. "Trying to stop Mom is like trying to stop a tornado. Don't worry about it. I'm a big girl. I'll be fine. Wayne is ancient history. Are you sure you're okay?"

"I'm fine," Roxie replied. "But I'm sure I look like hell."

"You look beautiful, baby sister," said Sinclair. It was true. Only Roxie could cry and still manage to look pretty.

"Let's go inside before Mom tries to find us," said Roxie.

At the thought of her mother, Sinclair braced herself. She loved her mother, but there were times when she could be a bit much to take. She knew that she was going to have to listen to another lecture from her mother before the night was through about the importance of finding a man. Frankly, that speech was starting to wear thin. Besides, her mom had never remarried, and apart from the occasional escorts to different social events, her mother didn't seem so keen on finding her own male company.

Chapter 2

Sinclair sat at the dinner table and tried to concentrate on her salad. Her appetite normally bordered on the voracious, but at that moment everything was tasting like cardboard. It didn't help that Ben Easington was sitting across from her, openly staring at her. It made her uncomfortable. It also turned her on. She hadn't thought about sex in a very long time, but she'd been fantasizing about Ben Easington since she met him. This was not good. Not good at all. The last time she'd felt this kind of attraction to a man, it had ended in heartache. She'd promised herself that she'd never allow herself to let a man have that kind of control over her again. But Sinclair recognized that Ben was not the kind of man to do things halfway. He would demand all of her, and that was something she couldn't give.

"What are you thinking about, baby girl?"

Sinclair turned to find her father slipping into the seat next to her.

"Nothing," Sinclair said and smiled at her dad. At

sixty, Cassius Dearheart was still a very handsome man. He was the color of warm copper, with sandy hair. His sea green eyes had a few laugh lines around them, but they only served to make him even more attractive. Tall, with a body that was kept lean by daily swims in the Atlantic Ocean, Cassius was still the heartbreaker his ex-wife had declared him to be. As a child, Sinclair had thought that her father was the most handsome man she'd ever seen. She'd been devastated when her parents divorced and Cassius moved back to Jamaica. Over the years, both Cassius and Sinclair had worked hard to bring back the closeness they'd shared, but the once or twice yearly visits to Jamaica and occasional phone calls hadn't quite allowed them to regain what they'd lost as a result of the divorce.

After Wayne left her, her father had come to New York to be with her. They'd spent a month traveling around Cape Cod, while Sinclair licked her wounds. Her dad had held her in his arms while she cried. He'd gently forced her to eat when food was the last thing on her mind. He'd listened as she'd railed about how Everett had treated her. More importantly, he'd also forced her to see that her life was still beautiful even if Everett had chosen not to be a part of her life anymore. He'd forced her to see the beauty in a Martha's Vineyard sunrise. He'd forced her to see the beauty in a child's laughter as she built sand castles at the beach. He'd forced her to see the strength in herself.

"This divorce will not break you," he'd said as they sat on the ferry taking them across to Martha's Vineyard. "It will hurt you, but it will not break you. No man should ever be given that power. Not even me."

When her father went back to Jamaica, she was still in pain, but her father had shown her something, something that she was able to hold on to during the terrible first months after her husband walked out. Her father had shown her hope. And she'd clung on to that hope even as Wayne told her that he'd never loved her, even as Wayne paraded her mistress around town before their separation was public. She'd clung to that hope even when Wayne tried to force her out of the house they'd bought when they were married. She now had a full life—a happy life. The wounds were still there, but she'd learned to live with them, just as she learned to live with the wounds from her parents' divorce.

"Where were you, Dad?" Sinclair asked her father.

Her father settled into his seat. "Hiding from your mother."

Sinclair grinned at him. "Did you succeed?"

Sinclair loved her mother, but her mother could be trying at times. When her parents divorced, Sinclair had blamed her mother. She'd believed that her mother's quest for perfection had driven her father away. In time, she'd come to see that while her father was a wonderful man, he was probably a man who should never have gotten married to anyone. A doctor, Cassius Dearheart was married to his work. No woman could compete. Not even his children could compete with Cassius's dedication to his chosen profession. That the marriage had lasted as long as it had, eleven years, was due in large part to her mother's stubborn determination to keep her family together. In the end, that was just not enough.

Cassius sighed. "As with every battle, your mother won. She found me and ordered me to come join the rest of the party."

Sinclair couldn't help laughing. Her mother had been upset when Roxie invited their father to the wedding, but ever since he'd arrived, she'd been ordering him around like a general ordered his troops.

"I'm glad she did," Sinclair replied, lifting her glass of wine and taking a sip.

"By the way"—her father lowered his voice—"the guy sitting across from us is really checking you out. Anything going on there?"

Sinclair almost choked on the wine.

"No! I just met the man," she whispered.

"Well," said her father as he picked up his fork, ready to dig into his salad, "he has good taste."

At that moment, Sinclair's mother, Belinda Rose, came to the table. The only empty seat was next to Cassius. Sinclair watched as her mother hesitated before sitting next to him. After all these years, her mother still was angry with her father. Sinclair had to admit that her mother could keep a grudge way past its expiration date.

Sometimes it was hard to remember that her parents had really been in love. Sinclair recalled a time when she'd come home to find them kissing on the couch. They were opposites, her parents. Her father was a workaholic who didn't care about social events or social status. Her mother was a firm fixture in the social scene in New York City, a grand dame who wielded her power like a cop wields his baton—with authority. Her mother came from money, and her father had been a scholarship student when they met at a party at Columbia University. Somehow, he'd convinced her to go out with him, and they'd fallen in love and got married, which was a big mistake. They were two people who didn't understand each other, even though they loved each other. They knew how to push each other's buttons, even without trying. The divorce had been bitter, and the end result was her father leaving the country.

Across the table, Ben Easington laughed. Sinclair watched as Marita, Roxie's college roommate, leaned over and whispered in Ben's ear. Marita was a known man-eater, as her last boyfriend, a record producer, had discovered. Apparently, Ben was successful or rich. Marita only went after big game. Still, by the way Ben Easington's lips curved in pleasure at whatever it was Marita was saying, it was apparent that he had shifted his attention from Sinclair to another. Sinclair was struck by an unexpected feeling of disappointment. Although she hadn't planned on acting on it, she was attracted to Ben Easington.

Sinclair's attention shifted as her mother stood up, her champagne glass lifted in the air.

Belinda Rose Dearheart's cultured voice announced to the room, "I'd like to make a toast to my darling daughter Roxanne Rose and to my future son-in-law Everett."

Sinclair shifted in her seat to get comfortable. Her mother was sentimental and loved the sound of her own voice. This toast was not going to be short and sweet.

Why Everett had placed him next to this gold digger would remain a mystery to Ben, since Marita was the kind of woman he usually ran from. He'd immediately picked up on her predatory stare when she'd walked up to him, holding out a well-manicured hand. He wanted to talk to Sinclair. His few attempts at talking to her at the table had been met with only monosyllabic responses. He'd been reduced to staring at her like a lovesick teenager. Marita was amusing, but her incessant chatter was getting on his nerves. Marita knew she was good-looking, and she wielded her good looks like a samurai wielded his sword. Another man would have been flattered by her attention, but all Ben wanted to do was get to know Sinclair better. He was going to have to find a way to gracefully divert Marita's attention elsewhere while he pursued Sinclair.

Ben watched as Sinclair listened attentively to her mother. Belinda Rose was an older version of her daughter. She shared the same dark brown skin as Sinclair. They were both tall, and they also had the same large, expressive eyes and high cheekbones. But Sinclair had a softness to her that was lacking in Belinda Rose. Ben decided if he ever went to war, he'd want Belinda Rose fighting with his troops. She appeared to be a woman who was tough and stubborn—someone with whose bad side he didn't want to be acquainted.

At that moment, Sinclair glanced over at him. He

winked at her and couldn't help the flash of attraction he felt even as she frowned back at him. She'd apparently pegged him as a womanizer. While it was true that he loved the company of women, he was loyal. Every woman that had been in his life could attest to that. People who cheated on others as a general rule could not be trusted—not in relationships or in business. He'd been raised by a father who'd taught him to respect women, and cheating just wasn't a part of respect. Somehow, he'd have to convince Sinclair that, despite appearances, he was a one-woman man. He'd decided that he was going to court Sinclair Dearheart.

He hadn't courted anyone in a while. Quite frankly, he hadn't had the interest or the time. His job as a journalist took him around the world, and apart from the occasional mild flirtation or, short dalliance, he'd been focused on his career. He supposed losing a family had largely contributed to his wanderlust. But lately, he'd been yearning for something that he couldn't quite put his finger on. He hadn't known what he'd been looking for until he saw Sinclair standing barefoot on the patio. He wanted someone in his life—someone special. He wanted Sinclair. He wasn't sure what it was that had happened in the time since he'd first met her, but there was something about her that made his heart recognize that he just might have found what he was looking for, he just might have found home. Now he just had to convince her to go out with him, and from the way she looked at him, he could tell that this wasn't going to be easy. Still, Ben wasn't a man who ran away from challenges.

Everett had told him that Sinclair had been in a

bad marriage. Well, Ben and Sinclair had that in common. Even if Everett hadn't given him that information, Ben would have recognized the hurt that was in her eyes. The way she looked at him, as if she expected nothing good from him, was born from pain. Someone had hurt her badly. Ben shook his head. What kind of idiot would let this woman slip through his fingers? He was going to show her all men weren't like her ex-husband. He just had to figure out how he was going to get his chance to do this.

He watched as something else besides a frown came over Sinclair's features. He watched as her eyes warmed as she looked at him. Whatever he was feeling, she was feeling, too. He smiled at her—a smile that held a promise of delicious things to come.

Cassius Dearheart was in love with his ex-wife. He'd thought that after everything he'd been through with that impossible woman, all his feelings for her would have disappeared, but apparently, his love for her had more staying power than he'd anticipated. He watched as Belinda Rose went on and on talking about Roxie, her family, and just how lucky Everett was to have their daughter's hand in marriage. This was supposed to be a toast, but as usual, Belinda Rose did things her own way. This quality still infuriated him. But it was this quality that had caused him to fall madly and irrevocably in love with her when he met her those many years ago at a law-school party at Columbia University. Although he'd been in medical school at Columbia, he'd worked as a bartender at the party to help pay for his expenses. He'd taken one look at the tall, slender dark woman with large brown eyes, and he'd fallen hard. She'd overlooked him at first, of course. Her snobbery was not one of her better qualities, but Cassius had been relentless. In the end she'd given him her number just to get him away from her, but somehow he convinced her to go on a date with him, and then, in short order, he convinced her to share her life with his.

Cassius smiled as he remembered their first date. He'd taken her to a jazz club in Harlem. At first, she'd been stiff, looking distinctly out of place with her long, pencil-thin skirt and her white shirt with a high-necked collar. She'd worn her long black hair pulled back in a severe bun. He suspected that she was deliberately trying to be the opposite of attractive. Her plan hadn't worked. From the moment he saw her, even until this present evening, he felt there was no one more beautiful than his Belinda Rose. There was also no one more annoying, infuriating, and, yes, intoxicating than his ex-wife.

When she'd asked for a divorce, he'd felt as if he'd been kicked in the gut. He knew that they'd been having problems, and he knew that Belinda Rose was unhappy, but he never thought she'd leave him. He knew that she still loved him, which made it all the more puzzling that she'd wanted out of the marriage. He was certain there was no one else. Belinda Rose was not the type of woman to engage in an extramarital affair. Cassius suspected that the reasons she gave him for leaving were truthful. She was fed up.

Looking back, he should have begged her to give him another chance. But the pride and hurt that engulfed him after his wife asked him to leave prevented him from doing what he should have done—fought like hell for his marriage and his family. He'd retreated to Jamaica, hoping that distance from Belinda Rose would help him get over her, but that hadn't been the case. Even though he threw himself into his work with a renewed vengeance, the ache that surrounded his heart when Belinda Rose ended the marriage was never far away. True, he never lacked for female companionship. Doctors, apparently no matter how old they were, were still in high demand with the ladies. And while he had come close to falling in love with other women, he still couldn't bring himself to make that final commitment. His heart still belonged to Belinda Rose, for better or for worse. *Damn her.*

Chapter 3

Sinclair fought the urge to breathe a sigh of relief as she watched the guests leave the wedding rehearsal dinner. She'd been ready to leave hours before. At thirty years of age, she still wasn't ready to face her mother's displeasure, so she'd made the best of a very uncomfortable evening. She was also worried about Roxie, who still seemed upset. So, Sinclair had remained through her mother's horrendous toast and had answered the inevitable questions from well-meaning friends of her mother, all inquiring when she was going to find someone special in her life. Sinclair had reminded them that she had someone special in her life—Princess, her faithful Yorkshire terrier. "What about a man?" her Aunt Cecille had gently inquired. "Been there, done that," had been Sinclair's response. Her aunt had rolled her eyes and said, "You're divorced, not dead."

Sinclair had felt her righteous indignation rise. She was a successful, independent woman. She didn't need a man. Just at that moment, Ben Easington had caught her eye, and for one treacherous moment, Sinclair wondered what it would be like to come home to a man like Ben. She wondered what it would feel like to have him wrap his arms around her. She wondered what he would be like in the grip of passion. From the moment Ben had stepped out on the patio, she'd been in turmoil. The blazing attraction she felt for this man disturbed her equilibrium. It wasn't bad enough that after a break of over a year, she'd have to face her ex-husband at her sister's wedding tomorrow. She now had to contend with a schoolgirl's crush on the handsome Ben. Unlike others who had been unlucky in love, she wasn't looking for round two; round one was bad enough, thank you very much.

Tearing her eyes away from Ben, Sinclair declared, "I don't need a man to be happy."

"I know you don't need a man to be happy, Sinclair, but you still have a lot of love inside you, no matter what Wayne did," replied Aunt Cecille. "Don't deprive some lucky man from getting all that love, Sinclair. Then Wayne would win."

"It's not a competition, Aunt Cecille."

Her aunt nodded her head. "True enough. But don't let that fool turn you into someone you're not."

"What's that?" Sinclair asked.

"Someone who's afraid to live life to its fullest."

"I have a very full life, thank you very much," Sinclair replied, hoping her defensiveness wasn't too obvious.

"I'm just saying, sometimes it's nice to hold someone at night, baby. I didn't mean to offend you."

Aunt Cecille was her favorite aunt. Although she was her mother's sister, she did not share her mother's social-climbing values. A public school

English teacher for the past forty years, Aunt Cecille and her husband, Uncle Harry, had provided a refuge for Sinclair when living with her mother sometimes was too stressful.

Sinclair gave her aunt a smile. "I'm fine, Aunt Cecille. Thanks for caring about me."

Her aunt leaned over and gave Sinclair a quick kiss on the cheek. "I better hurry up and get Harry up out of here. He's gotten a little liquor into him, and Lord knows, he doesn't know how to handle alcohol. There's no telling what he's liable to do."

Sinclair laughed and kissed her aunt good-bye. Turning, she came face-to-face with Ben.

"I've been awarded the pleasure of seeing you home," he said, with a slow and positively indecent smile. He was looking at her as if she were his favorite flavor of ice cream.

"Thanks, but that won't be necessary," Sinclair replied. "Everett and Roxie are going to give me a ride home."

Ben's smile widened. "Apparently, they want some alone time. Surely, you can understand that."

Sinclair's eyes narrowed as she looked at him. This smelled like a setup. "I can go with my mother."

"She lives in New Rochelle. Do you really want her to drop you off in Manhattan and then come back to Westchester?"

"I can go with my dad."

"He just left."

Running out of excuses not to ride home with him, Sinclair said, "I'll just take a cab."

"By the time you call a cab and it gets here, it'll be at least an hour. Then, you have another hour's ride to Manhattan. It's close to midnight. Do you really want to get home at two in the morning?"

He had a point there.

As if he sensed her hesitation, Ben leaned closer and whispered in her ear. "Your virtue is safe with me."

If he had any sense, he'd be worried about his own virtue, Sinclair thought crossly, but unless she wanted to wait an hour for a cab ride, Ben's offer to give her a ride home was the way to go. Besides, she was tired and her feet hurt from spending the evening in her cute, but uncomfortable, high-heel sandals.

"Fine," said Sinclair, conceding defeat. "I live on Seventy-second Street, off Broadway."

"We're practically neighbors. I live at Eighty-sixth and Columbus Avenue."

After saying good-bye to her mother, Roxie, and the few remaining guests, Sinclair walked out of the country club with Ben. He placed one hand at the small of her back, ushering her toward the valet section. They waited in silence while the valet went to retrieve Ben's car.

Sinclair tried to calm herself while they waited. It wasn't like her to be this nervous around anyone, but she was determined to get the reliable, steady Sinclair back in check.

A few minutes later, the valet pulled up in Ben's gleaming black two-seater Mercedes Benz. Ben tipped the valet, then ushered Sinclair to his car. Opening her door first, he waited until she was seated before closing the door and walking over to the driver's side of the car.

Being beside him in his car felt almost as intimate

as being in a bedroom. She strapped on her seat belt and tried to get comfortable. The car smelled like warm leather. Ben turned on the radio to a jazz station and then turned to face her.

"Look," he said, a small smile playing around his lips. "Let's just get this over with."

"What?" she asked, confused. "Get what over with?"

"This," he said, and before she could stop him, he leaned over and kissed her lightly on her lips.

The attraction that had been simmering on low all evening blazed, escalating to a five-alarm fire with that kiss. Her passionate response to his kiss took Sinclair by surprise. She wanted to attack him right there in his two-seater.

"I had to find out if your lips tasted as good as I thought they would," Ben murmured.

In spite of herself, Sinclair asked, "Did they?"

Ben turned on the ignition before answering. "Better," he replied. "Much, much better."

Cassius was waiting for Belinda Rose in her doorway when she arrived home. He was sitting on her front porch like he belonged there. Belinda Rose fought the feelings of annoyance and attraction that she always felt when she saw the father of her children. What on earth was he doing at her home? If he'd come to start some trouble, she didn't have the time or the inclination to deal with it. They'd argued at the rehearsal dinner about her decision to invite Wayne to the wedding. True, Wayne had done their daughter wrong, and while she didn't condone infidelity, Belinda Rose had always thought that her daughter hadn't fought hard enough to keep her man. Belinda Rose hadn't ended her marriage without trying to fight for it. Sinclair had thrown up her hands and let her man, her very successful man, walk away. In her heart, she was certain that Wayne still had feelings for Sinclair.

Of course, Cassius hadn't seen things that way. He accused Belinda Rose of meddling and being insensitive. Well, at least he was consistent. He'd never agreed with anything she did, which was why they were no longer together. She watched as he stood when she walked up the front steps to the porch. After all this time, he still looked good. He'd kept his lean physique, although to her eyes, he looked a little too thin. She couldn't make out the expression on his face. He looked troubled, but there was also something else there—something she couldn't put her finger on. Well, it wasn't her job to comfort Cassius anymore. She wondered, with a sudden stab of jealousy, who was comforting him now. Like her, he'd never remarried, but a man that good-looking was certain to have female company.

"What are you doing here?" Belinda Rose got straight to the point.

"Waiting for you."

"Why?"

"I want to talk some sense into you," he replied. "It's not too late to call Wayne and suggest to him that he not come tomorrow. He's caused Sinclair enough pain."

"We've been through this before," Belinda Rose

said as she used her key to open the front door. "It's late. I'm tired. Go away."

Belinda Rose walked inside, and her ex-husband followed her, closing the door behind him.

"I would call the bastard myself," said Cassius, "but I know he won't listen to me. You're the only one in the family that he apparently listens to."

Belinda Rose spun angrily to face Cassius. How dare he waltz back into her life and tell her what to do. Had he put the family first, they never would have been divorced, and Sinclair would have been better able to deal with the men in her life. With an absent father, it wasn't any wonder that she didn't understand men.

"Get out," she whispered. "Get out of my home."

"You ordered me out of your home once before," Cassius hissed. "Are you sure you want to make the same mistake twice?"

His words hit their intended mark.

Belinda Rose clenched her fists in anger and frustration. Cassius had always known how to push her buttons and then some. She remembered the quarrels they used to have. There had been more than one occasion that she'd flung china at his head. Thankfully, she had a bad aim, and she'd never actually hit him, but she'd come close.

"It wasn't a mistake then, and it isn't a mistake now," she said through clenched teeth.

"You know it was!" Cassius raised his voice.

His apparent lack of self-control took Belinda Rose by surprise. Cassius was always a man who kept his emotions firmly in check. She could count on one hand the times he'd yelled at her, but he was yelling now.

"You've said enough, thank you very much," Belinda Rose replied, keeping her voice level. She was tired of this argument, and she was tired of Cassius.

"I haven't said enough, Belle."

He hadn't used that nickname in years.

The air crackled with tension as Cassius walked over to her, grabbing her shoulders.

Belinda Rose was never one to back down from a fight. "What are you going to do?" she hissed.

"I'm going to kiss you," he said, his voice low and deliberate.

"Are you crazy!"

"Yes," Cassius said, right before his lips crashed down on hers. "Insane."

Belinda Rose struggled for a moment, but the struggle only intensified the kiss. Lord, she'd forgotten what Cassius's kisses were like. They were like a potent drug that robbed her of all good sense. She grabbed his shirt collar and pulled him closer to her. She wanted to feel his body next to hers. She wanted to feel his heart beat. She wanted to drink him in. Belinda Rose matched his passion as their tongues engaged in a familiar, and oh so sweet, mating ritual.

She didn't know how long she stood there, holding him, kissing him, touching him—all the while losing her mind. This was Cassius, her ex-husband, her enemy, who was kissing her senseless. She moaned into his mouth. This was madness. Surely, the two glasses of champagne had gone straight to her head. "Stop!" she wanted to yell out. Then she wanted to yell, "Don't stop. Ever." She felt Cassius's hands caress her—her shoulders, her neck, her breasts, her back, her thighs—and her last remnants of self-control were eviscerated.

He pulled his lips away from hers. "Woman, you drive me absolutely crazy," he whispered hoarsely into her hair.

"I hate you, Cassius," she whispered back.

He held her tighter, his voice fierce when he responded. "You don't hate me."

"Yes." She spoke louder now. "I hate you!" *I hate you for not realizing that your family needed you. I hate you for not trying harder to save our marriage. I hate you for coming into that party that day long ago and making me love you. I hate you for shattering our dreams. I hate you.*

Belinda Rose started pulling away. She couldn't let Cassius into her heart again. She couldn't let herself be seduced by his kisses, his urgent words, his passion, his need. She couldn't let Cassius back in.

Cassius pulled her back to him. "I'm not letting you go, sweet one."

Belinda Rose felt something hard and brittle inside her shatter. Feelings she'd thought had died a fiery death arose in her as she murmured his name over and over and over again. "Cassius. Cassius. Cassius. Cassius."

He scooped Belinda Rose up in his arms and carried her upstairs.

"I hate you," Belinda Rose kept whispering, trying to convince herself that this was true. She could feel his heart hammering in his chest, just as it had on their first night together. She felt the tears sting in her eyes. "I hate you."

"No, you don't," he replied. "You don't hate me."

Somehow he found her bedroom. Somehow, she was lying naked next to her ex-husband. Somehow, the tears were spilling down her face, even as Cassius kissed those tears with gentle lips.

It had been a long time since she'd shared a bed with a man. It had been even longer since she'd shared a bed with Cassius. A sudden feeling of self-consciousness washed over her.

She tore her lips from his. "Turn off the lights," Belinda Rose demanded.

Cassius shook his head. "I want to see every beautiful inch of you."

He made love to her slowly and deliberately, all the while staring directly into her eyes. "You're beautiful," he told her while he stroked her insides. "You. Are. Beautiful."

Belinda Rose knew this was his passion talking. She was almost sixty, and although she exercised and she'd kept her slim frame, two children and a whole lot of years later had taken their toll on her body. She watched his face as he entered her and felt hot tears roll down her cheeks again. They could never be the way they were before—the way they were when they first met and fell in love. They'd had so much hope for the future, for their future together. Belinda Rose grieved for what might have been. Their time had come and gone. Too much water had gone under the bridge. There was too much hurt on both sides.

Cassius kissed every tear away as he told her in urgent tones what he was going to do to her, with her, for her, before the night was through. "Don't cry, sweet one," he urged.

Looking into his beautiful face, the face that she'd fallen in love with so long ago, the face of her children's father, the face of the only man she'd ever loved, she felt a strange possessiveness come over her. He belonged with her. He belonged with her children. But, she knew in her heart that could never be.

Don't think, Belinda Rose ordered herself. *Don't think. Just for tonight, let yourself be loved by Cassius. Just for tonight.* Holding him closer, she joined him as they guided each other to an unexpectedly sweet climax. He screamed out her name even as they came together, spiraled out of control, and came together again. Afterwards, she lay quietly in his arms and listened to his steady breathing until she fell into a deep sleep.

"I take it you're not going to ask me upstairs," Ben said to Sinclair. After a largely quiet ride, where each person seemed locked in their own thoughts, Ben parked his car in front of Sinclair's apartment building.

She turned and looked at him, giving him an amused smile. "That would be a correct assumption," Sinclair replied.

Sinclair was a beautiful woman, but it wasn't just her looks that attracted him to her. There was an innocence about her that he'd rarely seen in a woman this good-looking. There was also a quality about her that made him feel protective of her. The way she looked at him told him that she was attracted to him, but she was scared of her own feelings. He would have to give her time to get to know him. He couldn't move in too fast or he would scare her. He wanted to kiss her, hell, he wanted to spend the night with her, but he needed to slow it down. The kiss they'd shared in his car was just an appetizer, a hint of things to come.

He watched as Sinclair unbuckled her seat belt. "Thanks for the ride," she said.

"My pleasure."

He didn't want her to leave. He wanted to stay in her presence just a little while longer. He wanted to know more about her.

"So you're a pet psychiatrist?" he asked, trying to delay her leaving the car.

"An animal behaviorist," she corrected, "among other things."

"Such as?" He knew the answer. Everett had filled him with exhaustive details about Sinclair.

"I own an animal clinic and a day care for dogs, and I have a weekly radio show."

Ben knew that he'd never get tired of hearing that husky voice.

"Everett tells me that you're the Pet Diva."

She smiled again. "The one and only."

"I'm going to have to tune in to your show sometime."

"Thanks again for the ride. I guess I'd better go upstairs and try to get some sleep before the big day."

Ben got out of the car and walked over to Sinclair's side of the car. He opened the door for her, and she left the vehicle.

"I'll walk you to the door," he said.

"Really, there's no need. I'm perfectly safe."

She was really nervous around him. The thought brought him a great deal of pleasure. She was going to run from him. But as fast as she could run, he could run faster. They would be together. It was only a matter of time. He wasn't an arrogant man, but he was a confident man. He was confident that Sinclair Dearheart was going to be a part of his life.

"My mother would be very upset if she knew that I took a young lady home but didn't walk her to her door."

Sinclair lowered her voice. "Well, we just won't tell her about your lapse in good manners."

Ben took her hand, lacing his fingers through hers. "The shame would keep me awake tonight, and you wouldn't want that, would you?"

"Let go of my hand," she said, staring directly into his eyes. He complied immediately.

"Okay, you can walk me to the door, but don't try to kiss me again," she warned.

Ben threw back his head and laughed. He could get used to spending a lot of time with Sinclair Dearheart.

Chapter 4

"What's going on with Mom and Dad?" Roxie asked Sinclair as she helped her get into her wedding dress. It was hard to believe that after all the planning, Roxie's wedding day was now here. Roxie and Sinclair were in a small dressing room at the Riverside Church, the site of Roxie's wedding. They'd both attended the Riverside Church, a stately and historic Morningside Heights church, when they were children. The tall white towers of the church still brought back memories of Sunday school, candlelight service, and the junior choir to Sinclair. Sinclair now attended a small Baptist church in Harlem, but in her heart, she was still a part of the Riverside community.

Sinclair buttoned the last button on the dress and stepped away to take a look at Roxie in all her glory. She looked stunning. The white, off-the-shoulder, satin Vera Wang wedding dress was simple and elegant. With a low-cut bodice that showed off Roxie's beautiful shoulders, a cinched waist, and full skirt, it made Roxie look like a princess—a worried princess. The tiny iridescent pearls sown on the bodice of the gown shimmered in the morning sunlight. Roxie's long brown curls cascaded around her shoulders as she turned in front of the full-length mirror and looked pensively at her reflection.

"You look beautiful, Sis," said Sinclair.

"Thanks," Roxie replied absently. Then, she said, "I'm worried about Mom and Dad. They're acting strange."

"Stranger than usual?" Sinclair joked.

"Actually, yes," said Roxie. "Mom is acting really moody, and Dad keeps staring at her."

Sinclair sighed. "Mom is *always* moody, and Dad always stares at Mom."

"Yes," Roxie agreed, "but today she's jumpier than usual, and the way Dad's looking at her . . . I think he's angry with her."

"Roxie, honey, they've been angry with each other since the divorce."

"I know, but this is different. I can't explain it, but this is very different."

"This is your wedding day," said Sinclair. "This is not a time to think about Mom and Dad and their drama. You should be happy. You're marrying the man of your dreams."

Roxie walked over to the window and stared out at the street below. She looked unbearably sad. This was not the way a bride was supposed to look on the morning of her wedding.

"Did you guys have a fight?" Sinclair asked.

Roxie shook her head. "Everett doesn't fight with me. He always lets me get my own way."

"That must be nice," Sinclair said, with a smile.

Roxie shrugged her shoulders.

Now, Sinclair was worried. Until the last week, Roxie had been deliriously happy about her wedding to Everett, but something had happened to change her outlook. Sinclair had been convinced that Roxie was just experiencing a case of prewedding nerves, but now, looking at her sister's sad face, she realized that something more serious was going on. She walked over to where her sister stood.

"What's going on?" Sinclair asked.

"I don't know," Roxie replied.

"Honey, if you're having second thoughts," Sinclair assured her sister, "it's not too late."

"I know," Roxie whispered.

"What's wrong?"

Roxie put her face in her hands and started to cry. Sinclair held her sister silently and let her cry. Something was very wrong, but her sister wasn't ready to talk about it. When Roxie finally stopped crying, she pulled away and asked Sinclair to get Everett.

"It's bad luck to see the groom before the wedding," Sinclair cautioned.

Roxie wiped her eyes with the back of her hand. "I need to see him. I can't marry him before I see him. There's something I have to tell him."

"Okay," said Sinclair. "I'll get him for you."

Belinda Rose sat in the small mother's dressing room at the church. She'd checked in on her daughters in their adjoining dressing room half an hour before, and although Roxie seemed a little nervous, she was certain that was just nerves. Roxie had always been a dramatic child, not like steady, dependable Sinclair. She loved both her daughters, but looking at them today, she couldn't help but wonder what she'd done wrong. They were good women, her daughters, but they had a quality that was foreign to Belinda Rose. Both of her daughters seemed to be afraid—afraid of life, afraid of taking chances. Belinda Rose understood that in Sinclair's case, divorce could break a person down. But years had passed, and that fear of giving love another chance still gripped Sinclair. Belinda Rose had been through divorce, and she knew intimately the pain that accompanied the severing of family ties, but she hadn't been afraid to love again. She'd made a choice to focus on her girls, and it had been the right choice. Sinclair was just plain old afraid, and Belinda Rose hadn't raised her to be that way.

As for Roxie, the girl was born fearful. Exams, spiders, dark nights, and relationships all caused Roxie to retreat within herself. Belinda Rose had been gratified when Roxie finally stopped running from man to man and settled on steady Everett. Everett was the right kind of man for Roxie. He loved her more than he loved himself, and Belinda Rose—who'd loved a man who turned out not to understand what love and family truly meant— knew that with Everett, Roxie wouldn't have the heartache that she'd had with Cassius. Still, the fear that she saw in Roxie's eyes had almost reduced her to tears. Roxie was afraid of the future.

Belinda Rose supposed that this was a quality shared by children of divorce, and she felt another stab of guilt. When she'd made the choice to end her relationship with Cassius, she'd felt that she was striking a blow of independence. She'd felt that she was showing her daughters that they didn't need to accept less from men, that they could go it on their own if the man wasn't right. But instead, the divorce had had the opposite effect on her daughters: they'd retreated into a world where their jaundiced view of men foreshadowed bad relationships.

That was why Belinda Rose had invited Wayne to the wedding. Even if Sinclair didn't want to get back with her ex-husband, she needed to face him. Belinda Rose understood that Cassius didn't understand this tough love, but Sinclair and Wayne had unfinished business, and Sinclair needed to put it to rest. Belinda Rose took a long, deep breath. *Calm down*, she ordered herself, even as she fought a rising panic. She still had unfinished business. She'd slept with her own ex-husband. Worse, she'd enjoyed sleeping with her ex-husband. This was nothing short of a catastrophe.

Belinda Rose looked at herself in the mirror. She looked about as bad as she felt. What on earth was wrong with her? Cassius had obviously preyed on her during a moment of unforgivable weakness. Even now, as the memories of what they'd done again and again last night flooded back to her, she felt a deep sense of shame. She absolutely hated weakness in anyone. She especially hated it in herself.

While it was true that women of a certain age still had needs, she didn't have to scrape the bottom of the barrel—which she most certainly had done when she allowed Cassius to touch her. Putting her face in her well-manicured hands, Belinda Rose let out a long groan. Who was she kidding? She'd enjoyed every single second of the time she'd shared with Cassius, and that only increased her shame.

When she'd awakened this morning and found herself lying naked in her ex-husband's arms, she'd let out a scream of dismay. Things had gone rapidly downhill from there. Heated words were exchanged when Cassius learned that Belinda Rose had no intention of withdrawing her invitation to Wayne to attend Roxie's wedding. Cassius was a skillful lover, but not skillful enough to change her mind once it was made up. They'd ended up arguing until Cassius threw up his hands in exasperation and stormed out of her home, but not before planting a firm kiss on her mouth. *Damn him!*

Cassius had no right to waltz back into her life and tell her what was best for her girls. She'd raised them largely single-handedly after he left. Now he had the nerve to show up and try to tell her how to handle her business. Belinda Rose took another long breath. She needed to pull herself together. This was her daughter's wedding day, and she would be damned a thousand times before she let Cassius Dearheart ruin this day for her. A brisk knock on the door interrupted her reverie.

"Come in," Belinda Rose called out, quickly composing herself.

Cassius entered the room, closing the door behind him. He was glaring at her. He was also looking at her as if he would scoop her up in his arms at any moment.

"I'm supposed to escort you down the aisle," he said, his voice curt.

"The wedding's not supposed to start for another

half an hour," Belinda Rose replied, pleased that her voice was calm, in contrast to the raging feelings that warred inside her. She was angry at him, and she was attracted to him at the same time. This was definitely not a good turn of events.

She watched as he jammed his hands into the pockets of his tuxedo jacket. He looked so dear to her—like an angry boy who was also impossibly cute. *Dammit. Dammit. Dammit.*

"I don't really see that it's necessary for us to walk down the aisle together," Belinda Rose continued. "We're divorced, for God's sake."

Cassius strode across the room and gripped her arms. Pulling her closer, he murmured, "That didn't matter last night, did it, Belinda Rose?"

She was so close to him that she could kiss him without moving. For a maddening moment, she toyed with the idea of kissing him. Then, good sense intervened. Tearing herself out of his grasp, she stepped back, putting distance between them.

"Last night," said Belinda Rose through clenched teeth, "was an aberration. It won't happen again."

She was annoyed to see him grin. "You and I both know better," he said.

Ignoring his taunt, she squared her shoulders. "Other than manhandling me, was there anything else you wanted to talk to me about?" Belinda Rose asked, happy to see a flash of annoyance replace his grin.

"Wayne is here," he growled. "I hope you're happy."

"I know what I'm doing," Belinda Rose replied, suddenly unsure about her decision to invite him. Wayne had called her six months ago, telling her what a mistake he'd made letting Sinclair go. She knew how lonely Sinclair was, and Sinclair also was a practical woman. Wayne was a handsome, successful man, and Sinclair could do worse. If he truly hadn't changed, Sinclair would see through that, and she'd move on. But, if Wayne had changed, then maybe Sinclair wouldn't end up being in the same lonely state that Belinda Rose now found herself. It was hard to admit that with all her social activities, her family obligations, her frequent travel to exotic locales, her various board memberships, Belinda Rose was lonely. She didn't want Sinclair to share the same fate. But what if Cassius was right? What if it was a big mistake to bring Wayne back into Sinclair's life?

"Do you know what you're doing, Belinda Rose?" Cassius asked her, looking directly into her eyes. "Those were the exact words you said when you asked for a divorce."

Belinda Rose tossed her head back in defiance. "I was right then, and I'm right now."

If only she could be sure on both of those counts.

Cassius's expression was inscrutable. "I hope you're right," he said before he strode out of the room.

Chapter 5

Ben sensed Sinclair's presence even before he turned to find her standing there in the wedding chapel. His breath caught in his throat as he took in the vision of her standing in front of him. She'd pinned her curls back from her face, exposing her large eyes. She was dressed in a pale blue, strapless dress that hugged her slim frame. On her feet were sandals that exposed the sexy toes he'd first glimpsed the night before. The red toenail polish she wore was a strong aphrodisiac. Slowly moving his eyes from her slim ankles upward, he took in the whole breathtaking view of her. The dress was simple, and it was set off by a pearl choker and pearl drop earrings. Pearls on any other woman didn't do much for him, but pearls around the slim neck of Sinclair Dearheart were indescribably sexy to him. Everything and everyone else faded away as Ben focused on Sinclair. He couldn't remember being this attracted to anyone else. Ever.

"You look spectacular," he said when he was certain that he could speak without croaking.

She narrowed her eyes. Obviously, his compliment was lost on her.

"Have you seen Everett?" she asked, abruptly looking around the chapel. Although the wedding wasn't scheduled to begin for another half an hour, the small chapel was starting to fill up.

"He's in back with the minister," Ben replied. Then, noticing the strain around Sinclair's eyes, he asked, "Is something wrong?"

She didn't answer but, instead, went back out of the chapel, in the direction of the minister's office. He followed her without asking. Weddings brought out the best and the worst. He'd been to some drama-filled weddings, and he hoped that Everett's big day would go smoothly.

She moved quickly, and Ben had to sprint to keep up with her. He grabbed her arm gently as she walked to the minister's office.

Spinning to look at him, she demanded, "Take your hands off me."

He let go. "What's wrong?" Ben asked.

"Nothing," she replied quickly. "Now could you just leave me alone?"

She was lying, and Ben saw right through her. Her eyes looked troubled.

"Look," Ben said. "Everett is my best friend, and all he's talked about for the last few months is his wedding. If something's wrong, I need to know."

He watched as anger flashed in Sinclair's eyes— a definite turn-on. "I don't have time for this," she declared. "Roxie wants to see Everett, and I need to bring him to her!"

Ben stepped back. "Okay," he said. Whatever was going on, he'd find out soon enough.

Sinclair turned and knocked on the minister's office door. Without waiting for a response, she pushed the door open. *Assertive and cute,* Ben thought. Sinclair Dearheart was going to have a tough time escaping from him. The more time he spent around her, the more attracted he was to this crazy pet psychiatrist—or animal behaviorist, as she'd corrected him last night. He followed her into the minister's office without invitation or hesitation.

Reverend Christie was a young minister with a very old soul. He looked like he'd just graduated from high school, but when he opened his mouth, he sounded like an old Baptist.

"Sister Sinclair," Reverend Christie's deep voice boomed. "And Brother Ben. What can we do for you two good people?"

Everett and the reverend were sitting in adjacent chairs. From their good-natured expressions, Ben determined that they'd just interrupted a pleasant conversation. Reverend Christie's office was filled with plaques and pictures of his wife and young daughter. Glancing at the pictures of the pretty brown-skinned girl, who looked like a clone of Reverend Christie, Ben felt as if he'd been kicked in the stomach. He thought about Africa, his own teenage daughter, whom he hadn't seen in seven months, and felt the familiar ache he felt whenever he thought about her.

"I need to talk with Everett," Sinclair said apologetically. "Roxie needs to see him."

Immediately, Everett's attention shifted to his future sister-in-law. "Is she okay?" he asked.

Ben watched as Sinclair gave Everett an unconvincing smile. "She's fine. She's just a little nervous, and she wants to see you for reassurance."

Reverend Christie laughed. "I see this all the time," he reassured the now-nervous Everett. "Marriage is a serious undertaking, and sometimes the seriousness of it hits folks right before they walk down the aisle."

"Where is she?" Everett asked, clearly worried.

"Follow me," said Sinclair.

Ben and Sinclair stood outside Roxie's dressing room as she spoke with Everett. Even though Sinclair had dropped several hints that she'd rather be alone, Ben stayed by her side.

It was disconcerting having him so near. It wasn't bad enough that her sister appeared to be having second thoughts minutes before her wedding and that her ex-husband was undoubtedly sitting downstairs with the rest of the guests. Now she had to contend with a raging attraction to an unsuitable man, Ben Easington. She knew his type. Handsome. Successful. Arrogant. A man who knew his appeal to the opposite sex and who took advantage of that knowledge—in other words, a man it was best to avoid. It didn't help matters that he was the most attractive man she'd seen in, well, forever.

"What's going on?" Ben asked, his voice surprisingly hard.

Sinclair turned to face him. "Could you please just go away?" she asked.

"Not until I know that Everett is okay," he replied.

He was loyal to his friend, she thought, both

pleased and surprised. She hadn't thought there was too much depth to be found in Ben, but she valued loyalty wherever she found it.

"I'm sure everything will be fine," Sinclair replied, although she wasn't quite sure of anything at this point. Roxie and Everett had been inside the dressing room for at least fifteen minutes. What were they doing?

At that moment, Sinclair's mother came walking toward them. Sinclair felt her heart sink. Her mother could smell trouble like a bloodhound could smell an escaped convict.

"What's the matter?" Belinda Rose asked. Her eyes raked over Ben and Sinclair. "Where is Roxie? The minister wants us to take our places."

"She's in the room with Everett," Sinclair replied, hoping to satisfy her mother's curiosity.

Her plan backfired terribly.

"What!" Belinda Rose screeched. "It's bad luck for a groom to see the bride before the wedding!"

Even though Sinclair had expressed the same sentiments, she tried to calm her mother down. "Mom, I'm surprised at you," she chided gently. "Surely, you don't believe in those old wives' tales."

Ben stepped into the conversation smoothly. "Mrs. Dearheart," he said, with a glib smile, "you're a vision! You're going to steal the show from the bride!"

Her mother's vanity was legendary in the family, and in the midst of her concern for Roxie, Belinda Rose beamed back at Ben. Sinclair rolled her eyes. As a child, she'd often asked the Lord why He'd sent her such a crazy mother. She was still waiting on the answer.

"Why, thank you, Ben. My own daughters haven't even noticed how good I look."

Sinclair felt her exasperation rising. "Mom, you know you look beautiful."

Belinda Rose stared at her daughter with piercing, speculative eyes. Raising her perfectly tweezed eyebrows, she said, "I know I look good, but it doesn't hurt to hear it from my own daughter."

Ben rescued Sinclair with the next comment. "I can see where Sinclair and Roxie get their good looks," he said, with an appreciative nod.

Sinclair watched as the compliment hit its vain mark. Her mother positively preened like a peacock. "I must say, you look pretty good yourself, Ben."

"Thank you," Ben replied, grinning at Belinda Rose.

Sinclair ground her teeth in frustration. What was going on with Roxie and Everett?

"Are you single?" Belinda Rose asked as Sinclair groaned inwardly. *Dear God,* she prayed. *Take me. Take me right now.*

Ben laughed and said, "Very single and very available."

"If only I was just a little younger or you were a little older," said Belinda Rose. She was openly flirting now. "But my daughter Sinclair is available!"

"Mom!" cried Sinclair. Embarrassment gripped her as she watched Ben's smile widen.

"I certainly hope so," said Ben.

Sinclair flashed him a look of annoyance. She would deal with him later. Then, she turned her attention back to Belinda Rose.

"I thought you were trying to get me back with Wayne," she said to her meddling mother.

Belinda Rose shrugged her shoulders. "It doesn't hurt to exercise all options, darling," she purred.

Before Sinclair could respond, the door to Roxie's dressing room opened, and a beaming Everett and Roxie emerged. Apparently, whatever crisis Roxie was facing had passed. She looked like a beautiful woman in love. She looked like a woman who was ready to get married.

Sinclair raised an inquiring eyebrow.

Roxie grinned back at her. "Everett loves me," she said. "And I love him. That's all that matters." Turning her attention back to Everett, Roxie linked her arm through his. "Let's get married, baby."

Apparently, Roxie's cold feet were now warm again. Sinclair looked over at Ben as he stared at Roxie and Everett. He looked worried.

"Okay," said Belinda Rose. She was back in command. "Let's get this party started . . . and, Roxie, what on earth were you thinking? You know it's bad luck for a groom to see his bride before the wedding!"

The wedding was uneventful but beautiful. The vows were said in clear, lovestruck voices by the bride and groom. Everyone held their peace at the appropriate part of the ceremony. Roxie and Sinclair's parents managed to sit next to each other during the service without killing each other. Ben, the best man, didn't lose the wedding ring. The two other bridesmaids did their appointed tasks during the ceremony with ease. The flowers, white roses and orchids, filled the chapel with a heavenly aroma. The candles, in their strategically placed candelabras, stayed lit. The

soloist from the Metropolitan Opera sang on key,
and Sinclair cried through the whole ceremony.
Even after her divorce, she still found weddings to be
unbearably beautiful occasions. Even though her
marriage hadn't worked out, she was still optimistic
about the state of holy matrimony for others. Even
the presence of her ex-husband, Wayne, didn't mar
the beauty of the wedding ceremony.

Throughout the wedding ceremony, Sinclair was
aware that Ben kept staring at her. During the few
times she allowed herself to glance in his direction,
she could see a mixture of humor and something
else, something undefinable, in his eyes. It looked
like desire, but she couldn't be sure. Still, the way
he stared at her, as if he wanted to possess her very
soul, sent shivers racing up her spine.

She had to admit that he was a beautiful man.
Everything about him, his high cheekbones, the
way his lips would curve into a slow, wicked smile
as he stared boldly at her—all of it was attractive to
her. He reminded her of a dashing prince with his
black tuxedo; ivory, cotton wing-collar shirt; and
black silk bow tie and cumberbund. He was distin-
guished, elegant, and just a little bit dangerous.
She imagined him sweeping her into his arms and
kissing her until she was breathless. *Stop it,* Sinclair
chided herself. *You're at your sister's wedding. The last
thing you need to be doing is dreaming about some handsome, commitment-phobic, globe-trotting man with dark
eyes.* From what Roxie had told her about Ben,
he'd successfully evaded commitment, while all
the time enjoying the attention of various females.
This particular thought brought an unexpected

feeling of jealousy. *Why on earth should I be jealous?* she chided herself.

Turning her attention back to the ceremony, Sinclair listened as her sister and Everett pledged their eternal love to each other. Looking at Roxie's serene, happy face as she repeated her vows to love, honor, and cherish her future husband, it was difficult to conjure up the near-hysterical Roxie she'd encountered before the ceremony began. Sinclair remembered that before her own wedding ceremony, she'd been nervous, for good reason, as she later discovered. But even with the wicked Wayne, Sinclair had been certain on her wedding day that he was the one she wanted to be with for the rest of her life. How wrong she'd been. But Roxie and Everett were different. She'd never met two people more suited for each other. Everett grounded the often head-in-the-clouds Roxie with his gentle devotion and practical nature. Roxie brought a softness to Everett, which was evident whenever they were around each other. Everett was a good man. Solid. True. Devoted. Kind. He was going to make Roxie a great husband.

The sound of a door closing in the back of the small chapel diverted Sinclair's attention, and that of everyone else, to the late-arriving Wayne. Her ex-husband had been late to his own wedding, so Sinclair wasn't surprised that he hadn't bothered to be on time for this wedding. Flashing an apologetic grin, he sat in the back row of the chapel. Sinclair couldn't help the feelings of annoyance that always accompanied her thoughts of Wayne. He was just trifling. There was no kinder way to put it. There were two occasions where, as far as Sinclair was concerned, one showed up on time—weddings and funerals. Knowing Wayne's large ego, she suspected that he'd wanted to make an appearance—which his late arrival accomplished. She fought the urge to shake her head in disgust. What had she ever seen in the selfish, self-absorbed man? True, the sex was good, but she'd learned after their breakup that good sex was not limited to Wayne Celestin.

Looking at her ex-husband, Sinclair was relieved to find that other than being mildly annoyed, she felt fine. There was no sense of aching loss, regret, or attraction. Even now, it was strange to look at someone she'd thought she loved so deeply and not feel anything at all, except a strong desire to escape that person's presence. It had almost killed her to leave Wayne. She'd been so afraid that no other man would ever love her. She'd allowed Wayne to convince her that no other man would ever find her attractive.

Although she hadn't met anyone that tempted her to open her heart, she'd been pleasantly surprised that there were men who didn't agree with Wayne's assessment of her. She was hopeful that at some point she'd let her guard down, but right now she was content with her life. She'd loved Wayne, but she wasn't sure she could love again—but she could have a good time, and she intended to do that—once the right man came along. Once again, her eyes strayed in the direction of Ben. He was staring at her again, causing her breath to catch in her throat. He seemed to enjoy making her uncomfortable. *Damn him.*

"You may now kiss your beautiful bride." The

minister's voice broke through Sinclair's tumultuous thoughts.

A spontaneous burst of applause erupted as Everett embraced his bride in a passionate kiss. She was happy for her sister. Despite Roxie's earlier misgivings, Sinclair was certain that Roxie had found her happily ever after. As Roxie hugged her husband, Sinclair felt the tears come to her eyes. She always cried at weddings. There was something so beautiful, so hopeful, about two people who loved each other enough to want to build their lives together. She thought about the children that would come from this union. She thought about her grandparents, particularly her grandmother Louise, who had come to live with their family after her parents split up. Her grandmother had been a stubborn romantic, filling both her granddaughters' heads with tales of love and loss. Her grandmother had gone to heaven at least ten years ago, but in Sinclair's heart, she felt that Louise was in heaven smiling. At least one of her granddaughters had found love. The tears spilled down her cheeks, and Sinclair wiped them away, embarrassed at her brazen display of sentimentality.

Looking over at her parents, who were sitting in the first row, she saw a sight that dried her tears almost immediately. Her parents were holding hands as they watched Roxie and Everett. Good Lord, the end was certainly near. This was certainly a sign of an apocalypse that was fast approaching. Her parents despised each other, and although there had seemed to be a cease-fire once the wedding ceremony began, this was something she never thought she'd ever see—a sign of true affection between her mother and her father. Her mother still referred to her father as "that Jamaican man," and her father usually avoided the topic of her mother altogether.

Her mother's eyes were shining with tears. This was surprising. Her mother had been dry-eyed at Sinclair's wedding, as if perhaps her mother had had some sort of maternal premonition that this particular marriage wasn't going to take. Her mother caught her eye and gave her a small smile. Then, as if realizing where she was and what she was doing, her mother pulled her hand away from her father's hand. Sinclair sighed. After a brief, magical moment, things had gone back to normal. She watched as her father's face hardened. Sinclair wanted to shake her mother and tell her to stop hurting her father. As a person well acquainted with pain, Sinclair recognized this quality in her father's eyes. Still, Sinclair knew that her mother wouldn't listen to reason, particularly when her father was involved.

After embracing Everett, Roxie turned and hugged Sinclair. "Thank you," she whispered.

"For what?" Sinclair asked her sister.

Roxie gave her a blinding smile. "For always being there when I need you."

Sinclair felt the tears well in her eyes as her throat tightened. Her bond with her sister had always been described as fierce. They were born three years apart, but from as early as she could remember, Sinclair had felt a love so fierce for Roxie that she knew she'd never let anything bad happen to her baby sister. Her sister at times had tried her patience with her inability to stick to her plans, her penchant for being late to just about every occasion, her habit of wearing Sinclair's clothes without first asking her permission, her continual fiscal irresponsibility, and her annoying habit of getting in Sinclair's personal business. But Sinclair knew that no matter her shortcomings, Roxie would always be there for her, just as she would be there for Roxie.

"Don't cry!" Roxie whispered, with a wide smile. "It'll ruin your make-up!"

Sinclair smiled back at her sister. "It was ruined a long time ago," she replied.

Everett pulled his bride back into his embrace, and Sinclair knew in her heart that this was one of the times in her life that she felt undiluted joy. Her sister was happy, and her sister was beloved. She watched as Roxie and Everett walked down the aisle.

Ben Easington held out his arm to escort her down the aisle, and once again Sinclair felt her heart skip. What was it about this man that made her act as if she'd lost all good sense?

She took his arm and gave him a steadying smile. He didn't need to know just how powerfully he affected her. He kept his voice low as they walked down the aisle together.

"You're a beautiful woman, Sinclair," he said.

She kept smiling and staring straight ahead as she replied, "I'll bet you say that to all the bridesmaids."

She was rewarded with a soft chuckle. Then, he murmured, "Just the ones that wear sexy red nail polish and have a great love for animals."

He was making fun of her career. Sinclair was used to people snickering when she told them that, among other things, she was an animal behaviorist, and she had a talk show devoted to the care of pets. But somehow the thought of Ben laughing at her stung her pride, even though she knew that she shouldn't care what Ben Easington thought of her. After all, after the wedding, she'd never see him again. She wanted to snatch her arm away, but Ben anticipated her move and just held on to her arm tighter.

Chapter 6

Roxie's wedding reception was held in the Crystal Room at Tavern on the Green. The romantic Central Park landmark was well known and was Roxie's first choice for her wedding reception. With its dramatic chandeliers, elegant murals of pastoral scenes, stained-glass windows, lit white votive candles, and pink, white, and coral rose table centerpieces, the Crystal Room opened onto one of the prettiest gardens in New York City. Sinclair had to admit that the setting was a perfect place for a wedding reception. As she watched Roxie and Everett walk around the room together, greeting their guests, Sinclair felt a sense of relief. Roxie and Everett were now married. After the months of planning, the fights with their mother, and Roxie's strange behavior right before the wedding, she was now a wife, something she'd wanted to be for a very long time.

After the afternoon feast—there were no other words to describe the vast amount of food—had been consumed and the various toasts had been made, the wedding guests took to the dance floor. Sinclair watched as the different couples danced to a slow love song and felt a sense of wistfulness wash over her. This was the part of the reception she dreaded—watching all the other couples dance. She loved dancing, and she'd often joked that one of the best parts of being married was never having to worry about having a dance partner. But those days were long gone. Her attention wandered over to her ex-husband, Wayne, and she watched as he danced indecently close to someone she assumed he'd just met at the wedding. Damn, he moved fast.

Although he'd come to the wedding reception alone, he never seemed to have any problems finding female company, which was one of the reasons they were no longer together. After the wedding, she and Wayne had exchanged a few polite words, but Sinclair had steered clear of him. Her mother's misguided attempts at reigniting their romance had failed miserably. Sinclair had to admit that Wayne still looked good. His cocoa brown skin was still smooth, and he'd kept his slim, athletic build. His conservative navy blue pin-striped suit reeked of money and fit him as if it had been tailored exclusively for his body, which it undoubtedly had been. But this expensive, conservative suit clashed with the diamond earring in his left ear and his gaudy, thick gold watch. He had always been flashy; that much hadn't changed.

Even now, she couldn't figure Wayne out. She'd thought that the flash was just a ploy Wayne used to throw people off guard. She'd been certain that lurking underneath his penchant for superficiality, there was a deep, sensitive man. After living with him and observing him over the years, Sinclair was now convinced that underneath the superficiality was just more superficiality. With Wayne, what you saw was definitely what you got. A Yale graduate and one of the most successful hip-hop music executives, Wayne had learned to navigate two very different worlds, the music industry and the hip-hop community, with apparent ease. Sinclair had to give the devil his due. Wayne was a very successful man. He just had difficulty with the whole monogamy thing.

"I'd pay a penny for your thoughts." A deep and now-familiar masculine voice interrupted Sinclair's thoughts. "In fact, I'd pay a whole dollar to find out what's putting that frown on your pretty face."

Ben eased into the vacant seat next to her. Suddenly, the temperature in the Crystal Room got a lot hotter.

"I'm not frowning," Sinclair replied, all too aware of just how close to her Ben was sitting. His knees touched hers, and that simple touch sent vibrations of pleasure throughout her body. She still didn't understand the effect that Ben Easington had on her. True, it had been a while since she'd been intimate with a man, but this wild urge to explore every part of his body with her lips was perplexing. She'd never thought of herself as a passionate woman, but her hands longed to run themselves all over his bare skin, like a sex-starved wanton.

Ben leaned closer and whispered, "You're making me blush. You're undressing me with your eyes."

Sinclair felt the blood drain from her face. Oh my God, he was a damn mind reader! How could he know what she was thinking about doing with him, and to him? She felt the frown that she'd denied having grow deeper.

He flashed her a wide smile. "I'm kidding, Sinclair! It's just wishful thinking on my part."

A small measure of relief came over her. Still, his words came very, very close to the truth.

"Do you know just how sexy you are, sitting there with that frown on your beautiful face?" he asked.

"Save your lines," Sinclair responded. "They won't work on me. I'm immune."

Ben looked directly into Sinclair's eyes. "So you say."

The heat between them made her uneasy. Maybe she was having an early hot flash, but from what she'd heard, hot flashes were not all that pleasant, and the heat that was infusing her was definitely a pleasurable experience.

"Look," Sinclair said, moving her chair away from him. "There are plenty of eligible women here who would love to hear your flattery. Why don't you go try your lines out on one of them? Believe me, your charm is wasted on me."

"Are you trying to convince me, or are you trying to convince yourself?"

"Hasn't anyone ever told you that arrogance is an unattractive trait?"

Ben grinned at her. "No one's ever complained before."

"Well, then," Sinclair said, "let me be the first."

"Dance with me."

"What?" Sinclair asked. Where had that come from?

"May I have this dance?" he asked. "I love this song."

The band was playing a rendition of Patti La-Belle's song "If Only You Knew." It was one of her favorite songs. She listened as the lead singer, who was good enough to record her own music, sang in a clear, strong contralto. *"If only you knew how much I do, do love you . . ."*

"No thanks."

"I'm not going to take no for an answer."

"I'm afraid you're going to have to—"

He interrupted her words by leaning close to her and giving her a light kiss. She felt a jolt of something electric and powerful hit her as their lips touched.

She stared at Ben. He looked just as shaken as she felt after this kiss. Sinclair licked her lips, still tasting his kiss. Everyone else in the room faded to black as she focused in on Ben Easington.

"Are you going to dance with me?" Ben asked, his voice hoarse.

"I'm guess I'm going to have to, if only to keep you from manhandling me," Sinclair replied, trying to tease him. She wasn't quite able to pull it off.

"I don't know what it is about you," said Ben. "But whenever I'm around you, I seem to be unable to control my urge to kiss you."

"You're going to have to try harder," Sinclair whispered, her eyes fixed on his lips.

He gave her another slow, wicked smile, which told her, most assuredly, that he was planning to kiss her again.

Sinclair stood up quickly. "Okay," she said in resignation. "Let's dance."

* * *

Ben was in trouble. Deep trouble. After success-fully avoiding all but pleasant flirtations when it came to women, he now found himself falling under the spell of Sinclair Dearheart. He couldn't describe it any other way. He felt as if he was intoxicated. From the moment he saw her standing on the patio, bare-foot, something had stirred in him that he thought had died—a powerful pull, an attraction, a need to get to know her deeper, an irresistible urge to be in her presence, a desire to protect her. He recognized the hurt in her eyes whenever she looked at her ex-husband. He wanted to push all that pain away. He wanted to show her that there were other kinds of men—men who didn't bring hurt and confusion. Men who would never let a woman like her go.

His friend Everett had filled him in on Sinclair's turbulent history with her ex-husband, and the more he'd heard about this fool, the angrier he'd gotten. Men like him made it hard for good men to get a chance, although, he thought with a rueful smile, it was obvious Sinclair didn't think that he was a good man. True, Ben had sowed enough wild oats to warrant Sinclair's or any other woman's mis-trust, but those days were long behind him. After the birth of his daughter, Africa, everything had turned around. He no longer wanted to be the kind of man that he'd keep Africa away from— men who broke hearts just as easily as they moved on. Ben had always been honest with the women in his life. He'd told them all that he was not the mar-rying kind, the kind of man who could stay in one place too long. That was the primary reason he'd become a journalist: it allowed him to make a good living while roaming the world.

Africa had made him want to be a better man. He'd changed his ways and made a promise to be there for his little girl, but as things turned out, his daughter's mother, Leneta, had been the one to run away. Leneta had been a one-night stand that had turned into a three-year relationship. Neither of them bargained for the child that came out of the relationship, but they both loved their daughter, and they tried to make their relationship work. After the relationship ended, Leneta promised to stay close so they could raise their daughter together. The ending of the relationship had been mutual in every sense of the word. Leneta wanted a man with a job that came with a large office, a briefcase, and a large sum of money. Ben wasn't sure what he wanted, but in his heart, he knew that he wanted something else. They remained friends, with Ben baby-sitting his daughter when Leneta went on dates. Ben still took the assignments that took him away from his daughter, but he made a pact never to be away from Africa longer than a week.

This arrangement suited him, and it suited Leneta until she fell in love, got married, and moved to California, taking his daughter with her. He was devastated. His daughter was his life, but he didn't try to stop Leneta from finding her happiness. He knew that she deserved to find a man who would marry her. Ben had never been able to take that final step. Leneta's husband was a good man who doted on her and who loved Africa. Still, the ache in his heart whenever Ben thought of Africa was never far away. He saw her on holidays, and during the summer, she'd spend a month with him, but it was never enough. Every minute they spent together, they had to relearn each other, and by the time they'd gotten comfortable with one another, it was time to go.

The years had flown by, and Africa was now fifteen years old. In many ways, she was a stranger to her father. She'd called him a few days ago, demanding that he send her money to buy a new computer. He'd sent her the money, but he was still waiting for a thank-you from his daughter. He knew that Africa resented him for being far away. He couldn't explain to her that it was her mother who'd left him and not the other way around. The guilt he felt for not being with his daughter translated into his spoiling her. He was determined that she would never want for any-thing. But he was beginning to wonder if maybe he'd gone overboard. Her grades, which normally were stellar, had slipped, and Leneta had informed him that Africa had been hanging out with some wild kids. He was going to have to talk to his daughter, but talking to a teenage girl required more skill than he obviously had. Usually when he tried to have a serious talk with Africa, she ended up in tears, and he ended up having a headache.

This wasn't what he had envisioned his family would be. He'd thought that if he ever had a child, he'd be raising his child with his woman by his side. He just hadn't met the right woman—a woman who fit in his arms just as perfectly as Sinclair Dear-heart. When he pulled her close during the dance, she resisted, holding herself rigidly apart from him, but he persisted and held her tight. As she gradu-ally relaxed, he found himself drinking in her scent. He tried to joke with her, to keep things light, but he knew that she felt the same attraction that he felt. He also knew that she was scared. Hell, he was scared, too. He hadn't ever felt this possessive or this protective about a woman.

He leaned down and whispered in her ear, "I want to see you again." Ben felt Sinclair stiffen after he said the words.

She shook her head. "That's not a good idea," she replied.

"Why not?"

"It just isn't."

"I disagree," he said, molding her body to his as they kept perfect time to the music.

"You're just horny," said Sinclair.

Ben threw back his head as his laughter erupted. He noticed several people, including Sinclair's ex-husband, look in their direction. When his laughter subsided, he said, "You noticed."

The evidence of his attraction had made its presence known almost as soon as he'd pulled her close to him.

Sinclair cleared her throat. "Hard not to notice," she said. "I have to say I'm flattered."

Ben grinned. "You should be," he replied.

"Modest, aren't you?" Sinclair chided him.

"An overrated virtue," Ben said, deliberately teasing her. He could get used to hearing that husky voice.

"I'm not so sure modesty is overrated," said Sinclair. "You might want to try it sometime."

Ben spun her around into a perfectly executed dip. "I wouldn't count on it."

* * *

After dancing with Ben, Sinclair walked back to her seat, glad to have escaped the dance without grabbing him and kissing him on the dance floor. She didn't know what it was about him that made all her common sense disappear. She'd always prided herself on being the stable, no-nonsense sister, but she'd flirted outrageously with him during the five songs they'd danced to. She'd enjoyed flirting with him, just as she'd enjoyed being in his arms.

Ben had disappeared with Everett to take pictures in the garden with the other groomsmen, promising to return for another dance. Sinclair couldn't help smiling. Ben had trouble written all over him, but it had been a long time since any man had held her interest, and Ben definitely had her interested—although she wasn't quite sure what she was interested in. Ben wasn't a long-term person, that much she could tell. She'd have fun with him, that was certain, but after the fun was over, would it have been worth it?

Across the room, she saw her ex-husband, Wayne, walking toward her. She felt her heart sink as he came closer. Wayne was the last person she wanted to speak with. She noticed curious stares in her direction. Many of the guests knew that they were divorced, and Sinclair was certain that there were quite a few folks present who wondered, knowing what Wayne had put her through, whether she would take off her light blue satin sandals and fling them at him in a dramatic hissy fit. They needn't have wondered; public scenes were not her style.

Wayne stood in front of her. "Mind if I sit

down?" he asked. His aftershave cologne was over-powering and not at all pleasant.

Sinclair shrugged her shoulders. "It's a free country."

He flashed a grin at her, and Sinclair found her-self growing cold. What on earth had she ever seen in him?

He sat in the empty seat beside her. "Baby, you still look good."

Sinclair looked directly into his eyes. "I'm not your baby."

Wayne's grin faltered as he narrowed his eyes. "You've gotten bitter," he said.

"No," Sinclair replied. "I've grown up. Divorce has a way of doing that."

Why had she said that to him? He still got to her. She didn't want to be with him, but she was still angry at him. He'd hurt her badly, and she wasn't quite ready to forgive and forget.

"You're the one that filed for divorce. I never wanted our marriage to end."

Sinclair forced herself to keep her voice under control. "You were cheating on me," she said calmly. "Once I found that little tidbit out, it was time to go."

Sinclair felt a momentary surge of pleasure to see that Wayne looked uncomfortable.

"Ancient history," he said. "I've found the Lord."

"Really?" Sinclair replied. "Where'd you find Him? In the strip clubs?"

Wayne narrowed his eyes again in annoyance. Her words had apparently hit a nerve. Wayne's ad-diction to strip clubs was just another bright red flag that Sinclair had ignored.

"I don't go to those places anymore," he said, but as he spoke, his eyes shifted to the left—a sure sign that he was lying. She knew him too well and for far too long not to recognize when he wasn't telling the truth. "Baby, we need to talk about us. I made a mistake letting you go. I had a long talk with your mother. Sinclair, I'm different. I know what I lost, and I want it back."

"It doesn't matter," Sinclair replied. She suddenly felt very tired. She wanted to be back in Ben's arms. She wanted to be with Ben. The few minutes alone with Wayne were enough to show her the difference between what was real and what was not. She didn't fool herself into thinking that Ben was a knight in shining armor. There were no knights coming to rescue her, no princes coming to sweep her away from life's unpleasantness. But Ben provided her with something that she knew she needed—something new. She'd already traveled down the road with Wayne, and the trip hadn't been worth the pain. She wasn't willing to go down that road again. Ever. "Whatever you lost with me, you're not ever going to get back. You didn't treat me right the first time around, and I'll be damned if I let you get a second crack at hurting me."

Sinclair stood up. Their conversation was over. "I really hope you find what you're looking for," she said to her ex-husband, "but it isn't me."

She walked away before Wayne had a chance to respond. Looking around the room for Ben, she found him in the garden, surrounded by two other groomsmen. He saw her, and something in his eyes made her footsteps falter. His unguarded look of pleasure when he stared at her scared Sinclair.

What was she doing? She didn't know him. All she knew was that he was Everett's friend, and that he was possibly the most beautiful man she'd ever seen, and that he danced really well, and when he held her in his arms, she felt safe and right.

She stood in the garden, watching as he excused himself from the other groomsmen. He walked over to where she stood.

"What's wrong?" he asked, searching her face.

She tried to smile, but she couldn't. She felt a rising panic as she tried to understand what was happening to her. She was attracted to Ben, and she was frightened by the powerful feelings that gripped her whenever she was around him. She knew in her heart that if she took the next step, things would change. She wasn't sure how things would change, but she knew that her life as she knew it would shift in a powerful way.

"Sinclair, what's wrong?" Ben asked her again. His voice was gentle, and the concern in his eyes touched her in a place deep inside that she'd locked away when she'd divorced Wayne.

"Nothing's wrong," Sinclair replied.

"Do you want to get out of here?" Ben asked.

Sinclair was finally able to smile. "I thought you'd never ask."

Chapter 7

Ben's high-rise apartment was a perfect reflection of him, Sinclair thought as she surveyed his home. Beautiful, understated, and slightly funky, it had floor-to-ceiling windows that afforded an almost unobstructed view of the West Side of Manhattan and the Hudson River, gleaming hardwood floors, expensive modern furniture, African paintings on the cream-colored walls, and brightly colored rugs that looked as if they came from South America or somewhere equally exotic.

Beside the living room was a full dining room, with a large mahogany table that could easily seat ten people, and its accompanying mahogany chairs, which had leopard upholstery, hand-carved lions' heads on top of the arms, and claw feet. The dining room led to a gleaming white and chrome kitchen, which was spotless. Sinclair was impressed. His home looked as if it came from the pages of one of those glossy furniture magazines that she always avoided. She thought of her own cramped one-bedroom apartment, complete with her mismatched furniture and clothes strewn across the floors of every room, along with the various toys her dog left around the house, and silently made a vow that she would clean up her act and start living like an adult and not like a rebellious teenager whose mother was away on vacation.

There were three bedrooms, which seemed odd for a bachelor, but it was obvious that Ben was wealthy, and how he chose to spend his money was his own business, Sinclair reasoned. The master bedroom literally took her breath away. Like the living room, the room had floor-to-ceiling windows, which added drama to an already dramatic space. The bedroom, with its vaulted ceilings and wood-burning fireplace, had a king-size antique sleigh bed, which dominated the room. There were several pictures of a very pretty brown-skinned girl. "My daughter, Africa," he'd explained, with a great deal of pride. "Where is she?" Sinclair had asked, but he hadn't answered. Instead, he'd changed the subject.

Ben had given her a tour of his home in an obvious attempt to ease the tension that was simmering between them. She'd thought that as soon as he walked through the door, he would have grabbed her and kissed her. But he'd been the perfect gentleman, offering her something to drink and then taking her by the hand as they walked through his place. She'd been curious about his relationship with his daughter, but the flicker of pain in his eyes, which he'd quickly camouflaged, when she asked about Africa convinced Sinclair to drop the subject.

After saying a quick good-bye to Roxie and Everett at the wedding reception, they'd come directly to his place. She'd been nervous, but Sinclair had been determined to see through whatever it was between them. She strongly suspected that she was about to have a one-night stand—something physical, nothing more, but she didn't care. She'd played by the rules before, and she'd gotten burned. She'd been a good girl, and she'd ended up with a bad boy. She knew that she'd probably be one of many women, but for once, she was going to abandon all good sense. She was going to follow her heart, or at least her libido. No one had ever looked at her the way Ben looked at her, as if he wanted to possess her, possess every part of her.

Whether it was a one-night stand or something more, Sinclair knew that any encounter with Ben Easington would change her in a fundamental way. She'd been in mourning since her divorce, and although she'd dated, she'd never let anyone in her private space. She'd always kept a part of herself secreted away, determined not to let anyone get close enough to hurt her again. She was going to feel what it felt like to let her guard down, and even if it was only for one night, she didn't care. She was going to have some fun. It was long overdue.

As she stood by the windows, looking out at the New York skyline, sipping a glass of wine that Ben had given her, Sinclair tried to think of anything other than Ben's close physical proximity to her. He stood close behind her, although he didn't touch her. She knew that he wanted her as much as she wanted him, but other than holding her hand when they walked through his apartment, he hadn't touched her. Night was beginning to fall, and the lights in the buildings scattered around Manhattan made her think of birthday candles on cakes.

Even though she'd grown up in New York City, she'd always felt that there was something almost magical about nightfall in Manhattan. Sinclair remembered spending countless nights staring out of her apartment window as the ink black sky blanketed the skyline and competed with the lights of the city. During those times, she'd let her imagination run wild, thinking of what it would be like to run away into the night, leaving all responsibility behind. She would dream that she was another person—a person whose parents were not going through divorce, a person who didn't always have to make good grades, a person who didn't have to look after everyone else, a person who could just be herself.

Sinclair turned and faced Ben. Here she was in this beautiful apartment, in this beautiful city, and with this beautiful man. She was scared, although she couldn't quite put her finger on what exactly was scaring her. She wanted Ben, and it was obvious that he wanted her, but she was scared. Had life done this to her? Was Wayne's betrayal the cause of her dry mouth and rapid heartbeat? When did she become this person who was afraid of living? When did she become this person who weighed the consequences of everything, from the calories of her favorite foods to whether she wanted to take off every stitch of clothing of the man standing before her?

Ben stood still, staring at her. "Make a move," she wanted to scream at him, but instead, she remained silent. She hadn't had much experience in the art of seduction. In her experience, it was usually the man who initiated things. Should she kiss him? Should she touch him? Should she get the hell out of his apartment, with her virtue and her pride intact? She was on the verge of running out of Ben's apartment, as her good old common sense had started to catch up with her, when she stared into Ben's dark eyes, and something inside her shattered. She was pretty sure it was her self-control.

It was now or never. Maybe it was time to do something wild that she could share with her grandchildren in years to come. Maybe it was time to act now and think later. Maybe it was time to have some fun in her life. Maybe it was time to find out just what it felt like to have Ben's arms around her. Maybe it was time to throw off the shroud of mourning. She licked her dry lips and asked, "Are you going to touch me?"

His expression changed instantly. There was an intensity in his direct stare that scared her. She saw a vein throb in his forehead. Suddenly, the tension that surrounded them was thick and uncomfortable. Perhaps she'd said the wrong thing.

"Do you want me to touch you?" he asked, his voice soft.

"Yes," she replied. God help her. It was the truth. "I do."

He moved as if in slow motion, reaching his arms out and gently pulling her to him. Sinclair felt her heart beating faster. This was unfamiliar territory. She hadn't slept with a man in over a year, and although her friends had assured her that it was like riding a bike, she wasn't so sure. When she'd been with Wayne, she hadn't been that confident in her sexual prowess, and after her divorce, what little confidence she'd had on that score had just about disappeared.

She fought the urge to pull out of his grasp, even as she wrapped her arms around him. Their lips found each other at the same instant, and everything else fell away. There was only this man and this moment. Sinclair could think of nothing else but the need to feel his hands over every single part of her body. This passion was all-consuming and nothing like she'd ever felt before.

Ben broke the kiss and stepped back from her. "Take off your clothes," he said. "I want to see all of you."

Sinclair shook her head. "You first."

The words that came out of her mouth belonged to someone other than her. These words belonged to a brazen, worldly woman, not a battle-scarred veteran from the broken-heart wars. She couldn't help smiling. Damn, it felt good to be brazen. It felt even better to be naughty.

Ben obliged and took off his clothes in front of her, letting his various articles of clothing hit the floor until he was as naked as the day God made him. Sinclair sucked in her breath as she stared at him in all his glory. To say that every brown inch of him was beautiful was an understatement. This was a man who took taking care of his body seriously. He was lean, and if he had any body fat on him, the naked eye couldn't detect it. Her eyes slid down from his dark eyes to his broad chest, his narrow hips, to the trail of hair that started just below his navel, and then below that. Her eyes widened as she saw the evidence of the effect she

was having on him, and then her eyes flew back
to his face. He was smiling now.

Running his eyes slowly over her, he said in an
amused drawl, "I believe the next move is yours."

She hesitated for a moment. Then, with a shrug,
she began to take all her clothes off in front of
Ben. He stared into her eyes and, like him, she let
her clothing drop to the floor. She hesitated again
when she'd stripped down to her underwear and
her bra. She watched as Ben's lips parted slightly.
He wasn't smiling anymore. Usually, she felt shy
about showing her body to anyone. Although
people regularly complimented her on her shape,
she knew her body's imperfections, and she wasn't
eager to share them. But, with uncharacteristic
boldness, she took off the rest of her clothes under
the steady gaze of Ben Easington.

Sinclair was timid about showing her body to
anyone partly because Wayne had been very critical
about her shape. Sinclair was slim and had never
had curves like Roxie. Wayne was a man who liked
big women, with big breasts. Wayne had never let
her forget it. He'd teased her about her small
breasts, and the jokes had hurt. In her heart, whenever she was with Wayne, she'd suspected that he
wanted someone very different. Tonight, however,
she was standing before a man who clearly adored
her body, and she reveled in that.

Ben began to explore her lips, her face, and the
rest of her body with his lips and his fingers as he
lowered her to the bed. A feeling of wild abandon
washed over her as she found herself exploring
him in return. When she reached the most sensitive part of him, she heard him utter a low moan,

and then he grabbed her, pulling her on top of him. Running his hands over her until he reached the place that had blossomed under his touch, he moved his fingers in a steady rhythm until she felt herself shatter as she screamed out his name in her sweet release.

Gently, he cradled her in his arms. When her heart had stopped slamming in her chest, and she found that her breath was not coming in hot, ragged gasps, she turned and said to him, with a mischievous smile, "I think it's your turn now."

She was rewarded by his wide, sexy smile. "I like how you think," Ben replied. "But unfortunately, we're going to have to wait for another time . . . I don't have any protection, and I'm assuming you don't, either."

"You'd be right in that assumption," Sinclair replied, feeling disappointed that things were not going to go any further. She'd been looking forward to round two. Still, she was glad that at least one of them had common sense. She'd been so caught up in the moment, she hadn't even thought about protection. "It's been a while since I've been with anyone."

He pulled her close to him and held her tight. "I'm glad to hear it," he said. "I don't like to share."

Sinclair snuggled in his arms, feeling as if she belonged there. "Neither do I," she said. She thought she heard him chuckle just as she drifted off into a delicious sleep.

Belinda Rose opened her front door. It was ten o'clock in the evening, and she'd just been settling into bed when her doorbell rang. She'd been tempted to ignore it; she was exhausted. But whoever had been ringing her doorbell had been insistent. She'd reluctantly gotten out of bed and walked downstairs to the front door. Looking through the peephole, she'd seen her ex-husband standing there. The last person she wanted to see was Cassius. The day had been stressful enough without adding her maddening ex-husband into the mix at this hour. The wedding had been beautiful and successful in every way. Her daughter had been a beautiful bride, the ceremony had been touching, the guests had raved about everything— from the church to the wedding reception at Tavern on the Green—but a feeling of melancholy had clung to her throughout the entire day. As happy as Roxie had seemed, Belinda Rose had detected some disquiet in her demeanor. Something was troubling Roxie, and beneath the brilliant smile she'd bestowed on everyone at the ceremony, Roxie, Belinda Rose knew, was worried about something.

Then, Belinda Rose's experiment with Sinclair and her ex-husband, Wayne, had failed miserably. Judging from the way Wayne had ogled the female guests, it was clear that particular leopard hadn't changed his spots. As much as she hated to admit it, Cassius had been right about Wayne all along. Wayne had been so convincing in his pleas to her to help him win Sinclair back, and Belinda Rose knew how lonely her daughter had been. She'd only had Sinclair's best interests at heart. She didn't want her daughter to end up like her— lonely and just a little bit sad. After Cassius, Belinda Rose hadn't let anyone into her heart, although there had been many potential suitors that came her way. Looking back, she wasn't sure what had made her run from a chance at happiness with another man, but she knew now that this had been a mistake, and she didn't want Sinclair to repeat history.

After she opened the door, she faced Cassius, the man she still loved and the man she could never have.

"What do you want?" Belinda Rose got straight to the point.

"Can I come in?" he asked. "I'll only stay for a few minutes."

Belinda Rose stepped aside and let Cassius walk by. He walked into the living room, and Belinda Rose closed the door and then followed him into the room.

"I just wanted to say good-bye," he said as he stared at her. It seemed as if he were waiting for a response, but Belinda Rose wasn't going to give him the satisfaction of knowing how much those inevitable words hurt her heart.

"You came over for that?" she replied. "You could have just called. You didn't need to make a special trip."

She thought she saw a flash of hurt cross his eyes, but it passed so quickly, she couldn't be sure.

He shrugged. "I just wanted to see you before I left."

"Why?" Belinda Rose asked, now curious.

He shrugged his shoulders again. "I wanted to talk to you about last night before I left."

Belinda Rose felt her legs go weak as images of

what they'd done the previous night came back to her. She was embarrassed that she'd let her inhibitions go and had let Cassius back into her private space, in more ways than she cared to remember. She sat down on the couch.

"I wish you'd just forget about last night," she said. "It was a mistake."

"A mistake?" Belinda Rose saw the anger rise in Cassius's eyes even as he spoke the words softly. "Is that what you think last night was, Belinda Rose?"

"Yes." Belinda Rose kept her voice strong, even as she felt the urge to run to him and hold him so tight, he would never leave again.

He looked at her without speaking for a second. Then he said, "You're a fool, Belinda Rose. A damn, stubborn fool."

Belinda Rose was inclined to agree, but if she was a fool, she'd be a safe fool. She wasn't going to let Cassius back into her life again. He hadn't changed, and neither had she. They'd only end up at the same place they'd been before—at each other's throats. They weren't good for each other. That hadn't changed.

"I'm taking the first flight out tomorrow to Montego Bay," he said.

Belinda Rose nodded, not trusting herself to speak. She wanted to cry, but she didn't want Cassius to see her being weak. She sat there silently, and it wasn't until after he left and she heard his car drive away that Belinda Rose burst into tears.

Chapter 8

The next morning Sinclair awoke entangled in the arms of Ben. She listened to his even breathing as he slept, and for a moment, she felt a rare feeling of contentment. Turning toward the clock on the oak dresser, she saw that it was just five o'clock in the morning. Although she was typically an early riser, this was early even for her. Moving slowly, she tried to maneuver herself out of the bed without waking Ben. As soon as she left his embrace, she heard him murmur in his sleep, but he didn't wake up.

She tiptoed out of the room and looked for the trail of her clothing in the living room. Finding her abandoned clothing, she dressed quickly. She knew it was cowardly to leave without saying good-bye, but she was going to take the coward's way out. Last night had been wonderful. She felt as if she'd crossed a threshold. She knew that no matter how bad she felt about how Wayne had betrayed her, she wasn't going back to him, and she knew in her heart that Ben was partly responsible for that. In the one night she'd spent with him, he had been gentle, he'd been passionate, and he'd been considerate. After being with Wayne for so many years, she'd forgotten that there were men who put her needs first—even in bed. She was never, ever going to settle for less.

After she dressed, she grabbed her pocketbook and left the apartment quickly. She knew that Ben would be angry, but she would explain later. At least, she hoped she'd have the chance to explain. She just needed to go home and be alone for a while. Ben was a man who would consume any woman he was with, and while she might have been ready for a one-night stand, she wasn't quite ready to be consumed. She wanted to gather her thoughts. She wanted to figure out just what she felt about Ben without the passion that flared up between them whenever he was in her presence. In her heart, she knew that although she hadn't known Ben that long, there was a potential that feelings could grow between them, and right now, she didn't trust her judgment. Although she was better than she'd been in a very long time, she still considered herself to be part of the walking wounded.

As she took the elevator downstairs, she fought her desire to run back up to Ben's apartment. The feeling of contentment she'd felt with him had disappeared immediately after she left his apartment. Now, all she could feel was anxiety as to what her next move should be regarding Ben. When she'd been at the wedding reception, she'd acted impulsively, perhaps even recklessly. Now, in the cold light of day, she wasn't exactly having second thoughts, but common sense had reared its ugly head, and it was telling her to go home, feed her dog, and do some serious thinking about Ben Easington.

They'd had a good time, but she wasn't ready to get involved with him. She didn't want to see him again. Ben was the kind of man she could get addicted to. She'd fought hard to get away from Wayne, and she wasn't ready to enter into something where she could end up getting hurt. As much as she'd convinced herself the night before, she wasn't the kind of woman who could sleep with a man and not expect anything else from him. She'd end up wanting more than just a good time—well, a really good time, a spectacular time—in the bedroom. At some point she'd want a commitment, or something resembling a commitment, and she was certain that Ben wasn't the commitment kind of man. He clearly wasn't the kind of man she was looking for. The kind of man she needed was an earnest librarian. Ben certainly didn't fit into that category.

His bride was gone. Everett read Roxie's note for the fifth time and tried to make sense of the words:

Dear Everett. I love you. I'm going away. I don't know when I'll be back. It's nothing you did. Please forgive me. Love always, Roxie.

When he'd awakened and found Roxie gone from the hotel room, he hadn't been unduly alarmed.

He'd figured maybe she'd gone to use the hotel gym; he knew that exercising for Roxie was almost a religious experience. She ran a mile every day, and her taut stomach attested to the five hundred sit-ups that she managed to do each morning. So, Everett had remained in bed, exhausted after a long night of lovemaking, for at least an hour and a half, drifting in and out of sleep. When he saw that it was almost nine o'clock, he'd gotten up and showered, feeling hungry and missing his sexy new wife. He hadn't found the note until after he'd showered and dressed. Then, his world came crashing down around him.

Sinclair's Yorkshire terrier, Princess, was not amused. Although Kiki, Sinclair's downstairs neighbor and resident pet sitter, had walked her the previous night and spent time spoiling her, Princess had obviously missed her mother. She'd continued alternately barking at Sinclair and staring balefully at her when she got back to the apartment. Sinclair had walked her, fed her, and even given her several of her favorite treats, but nothing had appeased Princess. Yorkies were temperamental dogs, given to high drama, and Princess was true to her breed.

After taking care of Princess, Sinclair took a long, hot bath and tried to get Ben out of her head. She missed him, which was nothing short of ridiculous, because honestly, she didn't really know the man. Well, that wasn't exactly true, but two days ago she hadn't even met Ben, and now all she did was think about him, or try not to think about him. Thoughts of the previous night's activities made her blush as she sank into the bathtub. She hadn't been a particularly loud or passionate lover in her past experiences, but last night she'd been both. She'd been brazen. She'd done everything but launch herself at him like a projectile missile. And he'd been a gentle, wonderful, and considerate almost-lover. She was glad that he'd kept his head together and stopped things before they went too far. Except for Wayne, she'd never slept with a man if she hadn't had protection, but dear heaven, she'd been ready to make love to him, anyway. *Not a smart move*, she chided herself. She knew better.

Princess continued to bark at her even as Sinclair tried to ignore her while she took her bath. After a few more minutes of Princess's high-pitched barking, Sinclair reluctantly got out of the bathtub.

"I'm sorry," she said to Princess as she dried herself with her favorite white, fluffy towel. "You already have a boyfriend. I was trying to see if *I* could get one."

It was indeed a sad state of affairs that Sinclair's dog had a better love life than she did. Princess's boyfriend, Blue, was a black cocker spaniel that belonged to Mr. Melosante in apartment 2B. Blue loved Princess with an unparalleled devotion. Princess barely tolerated him at times, and at other times, she would whine mercilessly until Sinclair would take her down to Mr. Melosante's apartment. As far as Sinclair knew, the relationship had never been consummated (Princess was fixed), but the dogs would spend time together playing or just lying contentedly beside each other when Princess was in the mood. At other times, when Princess's mood was decidedly different, she would lie across the room, staring at Blue with such disdain that the poor cocker spaniel would just hang his head down low, unsure of whatever it was he did to just annoy Miss Princess.

Princess was definitely annoyed with Sinclair now. As an animal behaviorist and a divorcée, Sinclair understood feelings of abandonment. Clearly, Princess had wanted her company, and she hadn't been too pleased to spend the night alone. Sinclair understood that also. When Wayne left, it had been difficult to sleep in the bed by herself. It was the only time she felt lonely. Although there hadn't been much touching in the bed in a very long time before Wayne left, she was used to having another body in bed with her. For the first year after the separation, Sinclair had slept on the couch, with Princess sleeping on the floor beside her. When she realized—and it took her a good year—that he really wasn't coming back, and what's more, he didn't need to ever come back, Sinclair had returned to her bed, and Princess had started sleeping in bed beside her.

It had all started so innocently, with Princess sleeping first on the floor in the bedroom. Then she would whine until Sinclair would place her at the foot of her bed. Sinclair knew that it was not a good thing to reward bad behavior, but Princess's persistent whining would wear her down. It was just a matter of time before Princess started sleeping on the pillow beside her. Sinclair had to admit that even though Princess snored, she rather liked the arrangement.

Sinclair put on her favorite Winnie the Pooh

pajama set and climbed into bed, with Princess still barking angrily at her. She knew that only a new toy, or some extended time spent with Princess in the park, would cause Princess to forgive her. Princess had a long memory, and she was particularly vindictive. She'd already peed in Sinclair's favorite pair of slippers. With Princess, retribution was generally swift.

"I'm sorry," Sinclair said again to her angry dog. "It's just that I met the most interesting and sexy man that I've met in years."

Princess was unimpressed. She kept barking.

"And he had the most beautiful brown eyes, and when he stared at me, it was all I could do to keep from ripping my clothes off and his."

Princess cocked her head to the side and stopped barking. This had clearly gotten her attention.

"And it's been so long since I've felt anything for anyone," Sinclair continued as she tried to get comfortable in her bed. She missed the feel of Ben's arms. She missed his scent. She missed his touch. She missed him.

Princess's left ear was raised. Her mouth was slightly open in anticipation. This was a sure sign that Sinclair had gotten her attention.

"And then we almost made love."

You slut! Princess's eyes showed her condemnation, or maybe it was just Sinclair's imagination. But Princess looked at her with clear, disapproving eyes.

Sinclair sighed. "It's easy for you to judge me," she continued. "You've got Blue. I don't have anyone."

Princess was still unimpressed, and equally disapproving. *If he's so good, why are you here with me?* Sinclair knew she was going crazy, because she was imagining having a two-sided conversation with an angry Yorkie.

"It's because I'm scared," Sinclair admitted. "I'm scared of what I feel about him. It's too intense. I hardly know him. Plus, one broken heart in a lifetime is more than enough. I know that Ben will break my heart. He's definitely a love 'em and leave 'em type. I just wanted to know how it would feel to lie in bed with him."

Princess raised both ears, as if to say, "I'm not good enough for you? We share a bed together."

Sinclair sighed. "Anyway, it was wonderful. And I got scared. And I'll probably never see him again."

Princess barked.

"At least I've got you, Princess," said Sinclair as she lifted Princess up and placed her on the pillow beside her.

Princess barked again. She seemed slightly mollified, but she still turned her back on Sinclair. In a moment, Princess was snoring. She'd fallen asleep.

Chapter 9

Sinclair was aware that her telephone had been ringing on and off for the last half an hour, but she couldn't bring herself to get up from her bed to answer it. She'd had delicious, erotic dreams full of images of Ben Easington. As wonderful as the dreams had been, Sinclair had to admit that, based on last night's activities, reality was even better. She tried to go back to sleep. The last dream had involved Ben, whipped cream, and a yacht floating on the impossibly blue Caribbean Sea. But Princess's barking and the constant ringing of the telephone eventually forced her to reach out and pick up the telephone receiver.

It was her mother. Belinda Rose was irate and verging on hysterical. Some mothers rose to the occasion in times of crisis. These kinds of mothers kept a cool head, even as all hell was breaking loose. They were the ones that lesser mortals leaned on: they could be depended on to give sound advice, to take charge when others faltered, to put all that had gone awry back into its rightful place. Belinda Rose was not one of these women. True, she was a fierce warrior, and Sinclair would hate to be the person who got in her mother's way if Belinda Rose really wanted something, but there were times when Belinda Rose seemed to forget that she was a strong woman, and she would fall dramatically and loudly apart. This was one of those times.

From what Sinclair could determine between her mother's screaming and her tears, Roxie had run off, and no one had any idea where she was. She hadn't been kidnapped. There was no foul play. Instead, after a wedding that had cost Belinda Rose a small fortune, her youngest daughter had decided that marriage to the man she had just recently wed was not for her.

"Has she called you?" Belinda Rose wailed.

"No," Sinclair replied. "I talked to her last night, and she seemed happy."

Belinda Rose stopped wailing long enough to comment. "It must have been a hell of a wedding night."

"Mom!" Sinclair chided. Honestly, her mother was born inappropriate and crazy.

Her mother continued. "I mean, it isn't as if she hasn't already sampled the goods. They were practically living together. What could he have done to make her run away!"

Sinclair took a deep breath. "Mom, this isn't the time for recriminations. We need to make sure that Roxie's okay."

"This is *all* your father's fault!" Belinda Rose had clearly left hysteria and was moving on to insanity.

"Mom, you're not suggesting that Dad encouraged Roxie to do this?"

"Not directly," her mother replied. "But his family is full of characters. Remember that sister of his that went insane?"

"Mom, I don't think you could call Aunt Beryl insane."

"She left medical school to roam around the world with that cult! No one heard from her for at least five years!"

"Mom, she's a nun now, for God's sake."

Her mother sighed. "That was after she lived a life of raising hell and bringing shame to her family! She's damn near seventy. She ought to have slowed down."

Sinclair shook her head. When her mother was like this, there was no reasoning with her.

"And his grandmother. Remember her? The one who used to let men draw naked pictures of her? Just plain craziness!"

Sinclair sighed and counted to ten. She knew her mother was upset, but right now she was worried about her sister, and her mother's mental break from reality wasn't helping.

"Mom, there are paintings of Dad's grandmother hanging in the Metropolitan Museum of Art."

"Naked pictures!" her mother screeched. "My family never acted this way! It's your father's genes that are the cause of this," she added darkly.

"Have you called any of her friends?" Sinclair asked, trying to change the subject to something more productive.

"Yes, both Everett and I have called everyone we can think of! She's gone and run off. She left

Everett a note. . . ." Her mother started crying again. She couldn't make out much of what her mother was saying after that, except periodically, she would hear her mother moan, "The shame," before bursting back into tears.

It wasn't that Sinclair wasn't sympathetic to her mother's tears, but although she kept trying, she couldn't calm her mother down.

"Mom, where are you? Are you home?" Sinclair asked.

"I'm home," her mother replied through her sobs.

"I'm coming over," Sinclair replied. "You're hysterical. You shouldn't be alone."

"I'm not hysterical!" her mother screeched. "I don't need you to baby-sit me! I need you to find your sister and bring her trifling self home!"

"I think you're being a little hard on her," said Sinclair, immediately coming to her sister's defense.

"A little hard on her!" Belinda Rose's voice rose at least two decibels. "She marries the poor man and then leaves him the day after the wedding! She doesn't even have the decency to talk to him. She leaves a note!"

Her mother did have a point there. It was cold-blooded to dump your new husband with a note. But it wasn't like Roxie to be so heartless. Something must have happened to scare her.

A feeling of alarm started to rise inside Sinclair. "Mom, you don't think that Everett hurt Sinclair, do you? . . . I mean, physically hurt her?"

Belinda Rose stopped crying long enough to give a dismissive snort. "Sinclair, get real! You've been watching too much Lifetime Television! Everett is the most agreeable man I've ever met . . . He would never do that to Roxie!"

"What—" Sinclair tried to respond to her mother, but now her doorbell was ringing. "Mom, there's someone at my door. I've got to go. I'll call you back."

"Maybe it's Roxie." Her mother sounded hopeful. "I always figured she'd get in touch with you first, although why she wouldn't call me, her own mother . . . Well, I just will never understand—"

"I'll call you back, Mom."

Sinclair placed the telephone receiver back into the cradle and walked out of her bedroom and to the front door.

"Who is it?" she called out.

"It's me," Ben's now-familiar voice responded. He sounded angry. "I'm here with Everett."

Sinclair opened the door and immediately regretted her hasty response. She was dressed in Winnie the Pooh pajamas, and her hair was all over her head. Not only did she look like some psychotic teenager, but she didn't have on any make-up, and her dog, Princess, was dancing around her feet and barking as if Ben were the very devil himself.

Ben ran his eyes over her. The passion that had been in his eyes when he'd looked at her before was gone. Instead, he looked angry. He looked very angry. In spite of herself, and the present circumstances, she felt a jolt of attraction as she looked at his mouth, which was now in a tight, hard line.

"Where's your sister?" Ben demanded, without so much as a hello or how are you.

Sinclair stepped aside. "Nice to see you, Ben. Come on in."

Ben walked in, and a clearly distraught Everett followed close behind. Sinclair felt a rush of sympathy as she looked at her brother-in-law. He'd been so happy the evening before. Brushing past Ben, Sinclair gave Everett a hug.

After she pulled away, she looked him in the eyes. "Everett, I am so sorry."

Everett tried to smile, but his lips only twitched. There were tears in his eyes.

"Sinclair, do you know anything about this?" Everett asked.

Sinclair shook her head. "No. Yesterday before the wedding, she seemed a little . . . off . . . but after you guys talked, everything seemed to be all right."

Everett walked over to her couch and sat down. Sinclair was suddenly embarrassed about her shabby surroundings. She had never been accused of being Suzy Homemaker; that had been one of Wayne's biggest complaints about her. But her living room, with its various magazines, dog toys, and jogging shorts from two days before strewn on the floor, looked like a storm had come through and paid a visit.

Princess kept barking, but now her attention was fixed solely on Ben.

"Can you shut this little rat up?" Ben asked, clearly irritated.

Sinclair bristled. He might be fine, and his kisses did leave her breathless, but how dare he insult her Princess. "Princess is a Yorkshire terrier. She is not a rat, but a wonderful dog and a faithful companion. Not only that, she comes from a long line of championship dogs. Her mother has won best in show at several competitions. Don't talk about her like that."

Ben jammed his fists in his jeans pockets. He was clearly exasperated. "I don't care if she knits cardigans, does the laundry, and plays a mean game of poker. Can you make her shut up!"

Sinclair narrowed her eyes as she looked at him. While it was true that she'd shared her first orgasm in two years with this man, that didn't give him the right to talk about Princess in that manner.

"Clearly, Princess is responding to your obvious antagonism," said Sinclair. "You are the only one that Princess is barking at . . . Obviously, the problem lies with you, and not with my dog."

"Sinclair, please don't be upset with Ben," said Everett. "He's upset about Roxie. We all are!"

Sinclair turned and faced Ben. "I know you're upset about my sister. Believe me, I'm upset, too. But I won't tolerate you coming here and speaking to me like that. And I certainly won't tolerate you talking about my dog. Believe me, I had no idea that Roxie would do this, and I'm worried sick about her. I want to find her, too."

Ben cleared his throat. "I'm sorry. I shouldn't speak to you like that."

"Damn right," Sinclair replied.

"Don't push it," Ben said softly, but she saw something close to admiration come across his face.

Sinclair turned her attention back to the irate Princess. "Princess," Sinclair said, snapping her fingers, "here. Now!"

There were times when Princess was openly defiant, but in general, she knew when Sinclair meant business. She stopped barking and marched over to Sinclair.

"Silence!" ordered Sinclair.

Princess cocked one ear, as if to say, "I know you're showing off, but I'll play along. For now." The dog stopped barking.

"Good dog," Sinclair soothed, reaching into a bag of dog treats that was on her couch. She took out a treat and gave it to a grateful Princess.

"Sit," Sinclair commanded.

Princess complied, knowing that another treat was coming her way. After Sinclair fed the now-quiet Yorkie two more treats, she turned her attention back to Everett. She ignored Ben, who stood in the corner of the room, surveying the scene much as she imagined a master observing his domain.

"When did she leave?" Sinclair asked.

"I'm not sure," Everett replied, raking his fingers through his hair in a distracted manner. "I know we fell asleep maybe a little after midnight . . . Then I woke up in the morning, and she was gone."

"Did you talk to anyone in the hotel about her leaving?" Sinclair asked.

"The night bellman seems to think that she left around five o'clock, but he can't be sure," said Everett.

"Are you telling us that you have *no idea* where your sister is?" Ben's hard voice cut into the conversation.

"I am not a liar," Sinclair replied calmly.

"Are you telling me that you wouldn't lie, even to protect your sister?" Ben asked softly, raising one eyebrow, which, in spite of her anger toward him, only made him seem irresistible. For one wild moment, she had the urge to run over to him and kiss him. She had certainly lost her mind, or maybe he'd worked some roots on her last night. Well, he'd worked something else, but that was an entirely different matter. She needed to keep her wits about her.

"As I said before, I have no reason to lie," Sinclair responded.

"Do you have any idea where she might have gone?" Everett asked. "She left a note, but she didn't say where she was going."

Sinclair shook her head. "What did the note say?"

"Just that she was sorry and she had to go away," Everett said.

Ben looked over at her, and for the first time since entering her apartment, he gave her something close to a smile, but Sinclair had a feeling that this was the kind of smile wolves gave right before they ate their prey for dinner.

"It seems you Dearheart women have a habit of running off," Ben said mildly, still smiling, although his smile didn't quite reach his eyes. "An annoying habit."

Either Everett didn't hear the comment or he chose to ignore it. Instead, he focused his attention on Princess, who was now sitting calmly in his lap, allowing him to stroke her.

Sinclair flashed a look of anger at Ben, but otherwise, she kept her mouth shut. Everett had enough on his mind without learning that his prim and proper sister-in-law had spent the night with his best friend. That was a secret she needed to carry to her grave. Judging from how Ben was treating her, it was clear that there would be no repeat performance of the previous night's activities.

The sound of the telephone ringing prevented Sinclair from dwelling on Ben. She answered the telephone on the second ring, glad for the distraction.

"Hello," Sinclair said, expecting to hear her mother's voice.

Instead, she heard Roxie's voice. "Sinclair, it's me," said Roxie. She sounded as if she was crying.

"Roxie!" Sinclair's voice rang out with relief. "Where are you? Everyone is worried sick about you! Everett is here—"

Roxie cut her off. "I can't talk to him!" she said, her voice anxious.

"Let me speak to her!" Everett said almost at the same time.

Sinclair shook her head in Everett's direction; then she turned her attention back to the conversation with her sister.

"Baby, where are you?" Sinclair asked.

"I'm in Miami," Roxie replied.

"Miami!" As far as Sinclair knew, Roxie had no friends or other connections in that city. "Roxie, what's going on?"

"I . . . I just have some thinking to do."

"Honey, you can't just run away and leave Everett. You're married now. . . ."

Roxie started crying. "I made a mistake."

Sinclair could tell by her sister's voice that she was scared.

"Everything's going to be all right," said Sinclair.

"No," Roxie cried. "I made a mess out of everything."

"Talk to me, Roxie," Sinclair tried to reach out to her sister. "What are you doing in Miami?"

"I'm on my way to Jamaica."

"Jamaica!"

"Aunt Beryl told me that I could spend some time at her place."

"You called the nunnery?" Sinclair asked, now clearly confused.

"She's not a nun anymore. She's running a bed-and-breakfast on the north coast."

"What?" Clearly, Sinclair hadn't been keeping up with the Jamaican side of the family. "When did you call Aunt Beryl?"

"She called me," Roxie said. "Yesterday, right before the wedding. She wanted to apologize for not coming. I told her what was going on. She paid for my ticket and told me that if I needed to get away, I could come to her place. So, I took her up on her offer."

"Does Dad know about this?" Sinclair asked.

"Heavens no!" Roxie replied. "He's going to kill me when he finds out."

"No, he won't," Sinclair said. "Mom's going to kill you. Dad will understand."

"I've got to go," said Roxie. "They're boarding my flight now. Tell Everett I love him. Tell him I'm sorry."

Then, she was gone.

Sinclair placed the receiver back in the cradle. Facing a distraught Everett, she said, "She's on her way to Jamaica. I don't know what's going on. She wanted me to tell you that she loves you and she's sorry."

"What did I do to cause this?" Everett asked, his voice raw with pain.

"You didn't do anything," said Sinclair. "And I know that she still loves you."

Ben spoke up. "Well, she's got a hell of a way of showing it."

"I'm going after her," said Everett, standing up.

"I don't think that's a good idea," said Sinclair.

"Sinclair, I love you, but I'm going after my wife," replied Everett. "If she's in trouble, I want to be there with her."

Ben spoke up again. "Man, are you *crazy?* This woman practically left you at the altar, and you're going to go running after her?"

"That's right," Everett replied, his tears suddenly gone. "She's my wife. My place is with her."

"Apparently, she doesn't see it that way," Ben said, still trying to talk some sense into his friend.

"I'm coming with you," said Sinclair.

"I'm not sure that's such a good idea, both of you running off to Jamaica. Maybe you should wait a while. She might come back," said Ben.

Everett shook his head. "I fight for what's mine," he said. "I'm going to fight for my marriage . . . and even if it doesn't work, it won't be because I gave up."

Sinclair watched the pain spring into Ben's eyes and then pass quickly away. Everett had clearly hit a nerve.

"I'll call my travel agent," said Sinclair. "I'm going to see if we can get on tomorrow morning's flight to Montego Bay."

Ben looked at her. "You're serious? You're both going to run after her?"

"She's my sister," said Sinclair. "Of course, I'm going to Jamaica. She needs me, and I'm going to be there for her."

Ben shrugged his shoulders. He knew when he was defeated. "Well, if you two are going, then so am I."

Everett spoke up quickly. "Ben, I appreciate your help. But Sinclair and I will handle this. You've got enough on your plate. . . ."

"I'm going with you," Ben replied, his voice determined and cool. "I'm your best friend, remember? I'm not going to let you face this alone."

"Of course, you should go!" Melody advised Sinclair after hearing about the runaway bride. "She needs you, and you should go to her. Don't worry about the show. I'll hold down the fort until you come back."

Sinclair gave Melody a heartfelt hug. They were sitting in the waiting room at the studio in the late afternoon. Sinclair's travel agent had made arrangements for the trip, which was scheduled for the next day.

"What are you going to do about your business?" Melody asked. "I can help out."

Sinclair smiled. "I've got that covered." Her business partner, Sylvester, had agreed to help out, and the rest of the small staff had volunteered to make sure that everything ran smoothly. She'd cancelled her appointments for therapy sessions with the pets. She was the only licensed animal behaviorist in the establishment. She hoped that her patients' owners would understand, and she was certain that all of them—except Hank, whose Siamese cat had the same neuroses that Hank possessed—would understand.

"Tell Roxie I'm going to put her on the prayer line," Melody said. Melody's church had a prayer line: the good people at Little Star Baptist would come together every Wednesday to pray for the needs of others.

"Thanks," Sinclair replied. "While you're at it, have them pray for me, too. Lord knows, when my mother finds out what I'm up to, she's going to lose her mind."

"You haven't told your mother?" Melody asked, clearly surprised.

"No, indeed," said Sinclair. "I'll call her when I get to Jamaica."

"Why won't you tell her now?"

"Because she'll insist on coming along, and the last thing Roxie needs is to have my hysterical mother berating her for running off."

Melody shook her head. "It must have been some wedding," she said. "Maybe when it's your turn, you should elope."

Sinclair laughed. "I'll never get married again."

"You know what they say," Melody replied. "Never is a long time. You might eat those words one day."

"I doubt it," said Sinclair as she got ready to leave the studio. She still had some packing to do, and she had to get her pet sitter, Kiki, some more dog food and toys for Princess. "Been there, done that. Got the battle scars to prove it."

"Don't let Wayne turn you against the whole male population," Melody replied.

"I'm not against them," said Sinclair. "I'm just not exactly *for* them, either. Besides, I don't see you rushing to the altar."

"Denzel Washington is already taken," Melody

quipped. "When they clone Denzel, you can dance at my wedding."

The next morning Ben found himself in the first-class cabin of Air Jamaica Flight 057, bound for Montego Bay. Beside him, a sleeping Sinclair shifted in her seat. She had protested when she'd found out that they were sitting next to each other, but the entire flight was full, and she overcame her obvious aversion to him and sat next to him, tight lipped and with a lot of attitude—not that he blamed her. He'd come on a little strong yesterday. First, he'd been pissed off when he'd awakened and found her gone. It had been a blow to his ego. He had wanted to wake up with her, dammit, but she'd obviously had other ideas. Then, Everett had come over, and after he'd heard what Roxie did, he went from being pissed off to being royally angry.

He was surprised at Roxie. She didn't seem to be the type that would pull a stunt like that. She seemed to be genuinely in love with Everett. God knows that Everett was crazy about her. He'd gone with Everett to Sinclair's house, and she'd opened the door, wearing the most ridiculous pair of pajamas he'd ever seen. For him, it was if she was wearing a sexy negligee: the effect on him was immediate. He wanted to have sex with her, and that pissed him off even more. Every time he was around Sinclair, his libido would rear its head, and it was all he could do to keep himself under control.

He stared at her sleeping profile. She was beautiful, but there was something else about her that tugged at his heart—an innocence that he hadn't seen in a very long time. This was a woman who didn't know how beautiful she was. She wasn't insecure about her looks, but she was simply unaware that when men looked at her, it often caused the same reaction as being punched in the gut. She took his breath away. She was beautiful and quirky, and for him, this was an irresistible combination. He didn't know how he was going to be around her without grabbing her and kissing her until she was completely senseless. He remembered the last time they'd kissed. He remembered how she'd thrown her head back when her passion overtook her. He remembered how she'd screamed his name as she found her release.

She opened her eyes, as if she knew he was staring at her. She blinked her eyes in confusion; then she frowned as she apparently remembered her present circumstances.

"Were you looking at me while I slept?" she asked, her voice cross.

He gave her a lazy smile, designed to infuriate her. "Yes," he replied. "I couldn't take my eyes off you." It was the truth. He could get used to staring at her till death did them part. Oh hell, where did that come from?

He watched as her brows slammed together in anger. "I can only imagine what perverted thoughts were racing around your head," she replied in disgust.

"You don't have to imagine," he said, with a wide smile. "I'll be happy to tell you all about it."

"Thanks," she replied, "but I think I'll pass on that particular pleasure."

"Is your father picking us up from the airport?"

Ben asked, quickly changing the subject as he sensed an uncomfortable tightness in his pants.

Sinclair shook her head. "No, he's sending his driver. He's on his way to my aunt's inn. Apparently, it's kind of remote and hard to get to. We'll meet him there later on in the afternoon."

"Why am I not surprised that it isn't going to be easy to reach your aunt's place? Are all the women in your family difficult?"

"Are all the men in your family jerks like you?"

"There was a time not too long ago that you didn't find being around me so difficult," he said slowly, deliberately baiting her.

He saw the embarrassment flood her face. "I wish you'd forget about that night," she said quickly, looking across the aisle at Everett, who was sleeping. "I was drunk."

He grinned at her. "Like hell you were. You were stone-cold sober. We both were."

"That chapter is closed," said Sinclair.

"So you say," Ben said, leaning closer to her.

"I mean it," Sinclair said, but her voice shook as she looked at him.

He hadn't meant to kiss her, but she had licked her lips, a sign of her nervousness, and that had been his undoing. He slid his lips across her lightly, and then he kissed her again.

"Don't do that," Sinclair said, her voice firmer.

"Okay," he replied, and then he kissed her again. This time the kiss was deeper. He probed her mouth with his tongue, and he felt his excitement rise as she responded to his kiss.

"My, my," said the male flight attendant in the

cabin, his voice amused. He had the accent of someone born and raised in Jamaica. "Newlyweds, eh?"

Sinclair pulled away from Ben. "No," she replied.

The flight attendant chuckled and moved down
the aisle.

"If you try that again, I'm changing seats," Sinclair hissed. "There are some open seats in coach."

"Don't worry. Everett didn't see us."

"Well, that's a good thing," said Sinclair. "But we
don't need to . . . take this . . . whatever this
is . . . any further."

"Who are you running from, Sinclair?" Ben
asked. "You running from me or from yourself?"

"I'm not running from anyone," Sinclair replied,
but her eyes were still wary when she looked at him.
Once again, Ben felt anger surge through him when
he thought about her ex-husband. He'd obviously
hurt her and even now, years after the divorce, the
remnants of that hurt remained.

"Good," Ben replied. "Because you and I are
going to be together, Sinclair. Right now, we have
some things to work out. But it doesn't make sense
to run from the inevitable."

Sinclair shrugged her shoulders, but her quick,
shallow breaths betrayed her turmoil. "The only
thing I'm concerned about is making sure my
sister's okay."

"I understand that," Ben replied. "And I respect that. I'll wait for you, Sinclair. I'm not going
anywhere."

Chapter 10

For the first time since she'd discovered that her sister was a runaway bride, Sinclair found herself relaxing. Jamaica had a habit of forcing folks to relax, despite their best intentions. There was something seductive, something calming, about this land filled with lush green hills, ubiquitous palm trees, verdant valleys, and the bright blue sea. This was the land of her ancestors, and Sinclair had always felt a strong connection to the land and its people, even though she'd never stayed on the island for longer than a few weeks when she visited her father. As she sat in the backseat of her father's dark blue Volvo sedan, even with Ben sitting close beside her, she felt a feeling of peace descend upon her.

The airplane ride had been stressful. Ben's presence had been unnerving, and his kisses had made a tense situation even tenser. Moreover, as a person who was well acquainted with broken hearts, she was touched by Everett's pain. She'd tried to talk with him during the plane ride, but Everett had been distant and noncommunicative. Sinclair couldn't blame him. Although she was certain that her sister had a damn good reason for her actions, she still couldn't understand how Roxie could have treated Everett in such a terrible way.

Once they landed at the Montego Bay airport, they'd easily navigated the long customs lines and the inspection of their baggage. They'd found Cordis, her father's driver, waiting for them just outside the customs room. It had been several years since she'd last seen Cordis, but he hadn't changed much. A small, thin man, the color of midnight, with long dreadlocks that hung down his back, Cordis was probably in his mid-sixties, but he looked like a man half his actual age. A former alcoholic and one of her father's patients, Cordis had been given a second chance at life by her father, and he'd worked for her father since that terrible time in his life. He was now one of the most good-natured men she'd had the pleasure of encountering. He had a perpetual smile on his face, and he was devoted to her father. Her father didn't need a driver, but Cordis had no real skills, and her father knew that without the steady employment, it wouldn't be too hard for Cordis to find himself back in the grips of his addiction.

As they drove along the narrow coastal highway that took them east from Montego Bay and toward the town of St. Christopher, in the parish of St. Ann, where her father lived, Sinclair found herself lost in memories of visiting the island when she was a child. She'd loved the colorful people, with their wonderful sayings and their rich history. As a child, she'd learned about the Maroons, former slaves who had fought the Europeans. She'd learned about Sir Alexander Bustamante, a distant relative, who'd helped Jamaica win its independence from the British Crown. She'd learned about the pirates who had ruled the Caribbean from the town of Port Royal, which had been almost entirely destroyed by an earthquake, taking most of its inhabitants and its ill-gotten gains into the sea. She'd been fascinated by the history of her people, and despite her mother's best attempts to distance her from her Jamaican relatives, Sinclair still felt a strong connection to this place.

Although she was still worried about her sister, she was equally worried about Everett, who sat stone-faced in the front of the vehicle, beside Cordis. She prayed that both Roxie and Everett would find their way back to each other. Despite her sister's actions, she knew that Rosie still loved Everett and Everett's love for Roxie remained strong despite his obvious pain. The wind that caressed her face through the open car window whispered to her that somehow things were going to turn out all right. Cordis had informed them that although her father had set out for her aunt's inn, he still hadn't reached it. Apparently, there had been a bad rainstorm, which had rendered the main road to the inn impassable. Her father had decided to spend the remainder of the day in Port Antonio, which was about twenty miles from Blue Horizons, her aunt's bed-and-breakfast.

"How soon will we get to your father's place?" Ben asked.

Cordis answered, "We'll be there in another hour, mon."

Everett finally spoke. "What's the plan once we

get there? I still think that we should go directly to the place where Roxie's staying."

Sinclair leaned forward and gave Everett's shoulder a sympathetic squeeze. "Dad thinks it's best that he go first to talk to her. Once that's done, we'll go directly to Blue Horizons."

"There's no guarantee that she won't run again," Everett said, worry making him sound testy.

Sinclair sighed. "There's no guarantee that she won't run once we get there. I think Dad's plan is the best we have for right now."

Everett was undeterred. "Why can't we call her?"

"Dad's in touch with her," Sinclair replied. "She told him that the only person she wants to talk to is him. For now, we're going to respect that."

Everett shook his head. He was apparently unconvinced.

Sinclair gave Everett's shoulder another squeeze. "Don't worry," she said. "If anyone can get through to Roxie, Dad can."

She heard a low chuckle come from Ben's direction, but she refused to look at him. She wouldn't give him the satisfaction. She knew Ben thought that their plan to come to Jamaica to get Roxie was crazy, but no one had asked him to tag along for the ride.

"You know," Sinclair said, speaking in a low voice so that only Ben could hear her, "if you didn't want to come along, you should have stayed in New York."

She heard him chuckle again. "And miss the chance to hang out with you while you race around a Caribbean island, trying to find a woman who obviously doesn't want to be found? I wouldn't miss this for the world."

Sinclair couldn't help the grimace that accompanied his words. "Lucky me," she replied, sarcasm dripping from her like a leaking faucet. Ben's response only made her grit her teeth in frustration.

"That's exactly what I think," Ben said, and the meaning behind his bland words was unmistakable. "You are a lucky woman."

Roxie sat on the veranda at Blue Horizons and watched the sun start its descent on the surrounding mountain range. Her aunt's inn was the perfect place for an escape from the harsh realities that faced her. It was remote and difficult to get to. Few people had heard of the inn, and Roxie's Aunt Beryl liked it that way. The majority of her guests were friends or had been referred to Blue Horizons by her friends. The inn was clearly not a moneymaking operation, but a labor of love.

Located in the interior of the island, surrounded by forests and mountain ranges, and accessible only by inhospitable dirt roads, the inn was well off the beaten track. The nearest town was at least twenty miles away, but it might as well have been a million miles. Roxie truly felt as if she were in the middle of nowhere. The inn was in reality a converted villa with six bedrooms. It consisted of three floors. The first floor contained a large and airy living room filled with native framed prints and sculptures. Beside the living room was a full dining room and small kitchen. The bedrooms and adjoining bathrooms were located on the upper floors. With the exception of a German couple on their honey-

moon and Roxie's aunt, the inn was deserted. The
month of August did not fall in the busy tourist
season in Jamaica, and Roxie was grateful. The last
thing she wanted to do was face happy people on
vacation. It was bad enough that there was a couple
on their honeymoon at the inn. She was supposed
to be on her own honeymoon in the Seychelle Is-
lands. Instead, she was sitting on her aunt's veranda,
brokenhearted and afraid, looking at the mountains and wondering how Everett was coping with
her sudden disappearance.

The thought of Everett brought more tears to her
eyes. Since she'd gotten on the island and her aunt
had picked her up from the airport, she'd been
crying. She'd thought that after a day and a half of
tears, she'd finally lose the capacity to continue
crying, but the tears still fell freely, especially when
she thought of what she'd done to Everett. He was a
good man who didn't deserve to be treated the way
she'd treated him. She'd taken the cowardly way out.
She'd married him, even though she knew she was
making the wrong choice. She loved him more than
she'd ever loved any man, but she'd done terrible
things to him.

When she awoke the day after the wedding,
she'd been gripped with a panic she could hardly
describe even now. She'd felt as if someone had
choked all the air out of her, and she couldn't
breathe. The sense that her world was about to
come crashing down around her and that her terrible secret would one day be revealed was too
much for her. She ran. But even though she'd run
far, the same panic that had strangled her yesterday continued—even in these beautiful and

remote surroundings. If anything, she felt worse, because, although she'd run away from her problem, she hadn't run away from herself, or from her demons.

She sat on one of the several white wicker chairs, with their brightly colored cushions, and tried to determine what her next move should be. Her aunt had told her that she could stay with her for as long as she liked, but under her present circumstances, she knew that this would be impossible. She could hear the melody of the wind chimes hanging on the veranda, as a cool breeze surrounded her. Closing her eyes, Roxie let the sounds of the wind chimes wash over her. She felt a momentary calm, but then her thoughts turned once again to her current situation, and she felt the now-familiar panic grab her.

"Here," a gentle voice urged. "Drink this lemonade. Life always looks a little better after a person has had some of my lemonade."

Roxie turned and found herself facing her smiling Aunt Beryl. She was holding out a glass of lemonade. Roxie took the glass from her aunt's hand, but she had no appetite, even for her aunt's legendary lemonade. At seventy years old, Beryl Dearheart Cuthbert Sangster was a knockout. Like Roxie's father, Beryl had copper-colored skin and green eyes. They also shared the same high cheekbones, full lips, pointed chin, and thin nose, with slightly flared nostrils. Beryl carried herself like a queen. She'd been married three times to interesting men, who all loved her even when she left them, and for a short period of time, she'd been a nun. She was now content to run her inn, grow her garden, and paint scenes of Jamaican nature, all of which she could survey from her backyard. She was prone to be dramatic, and she tended to wear black. That evening Beryl was wearing a loose-fitting black cotton dress and black espadrilles.

Roxie tried to smile, but she just couldn't pull that off. She watched as her aunt Beryl sat down in the wicker chair next to her. Her aunt had been a godsend. She'd welcomed Roxie with open arms and no questions. Unlike the rest of her family, who no doubt stood in severe judgment over Roxie's actions, Aunt Beryl had made no comments. However, Roxie guessed that her aunt's silence on the subject of her runaway act was about to end.

"There's something about those mountains that tends to heal even the weariest soul," Aunt Beryl commented after a few moments of silence.

Ordinarily, Roxie would have been inclined to agree, but even the dramatic beauty of the Look Behind Mountains, as the mountain range surrounding her aunt's property was called, with their almost dark blue hue and the mists that crowned their peaks, failed to do anything but mock Roxie's sadness. Roxie remained silent.

"After my last divorce," Aunt Beryl continued, "I ran away and found myself here. I never looked back."

Roxie sighed. "That sounds like a good plan for me."

Aunt Beryl turned and faced Roxie. "Does it sound like a good plan?" she asked.

"It worked for you," Roxie replied, fearing that the tears that were so close to the surface would start again.

"You and I are very different," Aunt Beryl commented. "I was at peace with my decision to leave my husbands. All of them."

Roxie tried to keep it together, but she felt a solitary tear roll down her cheek. "I had no choice," she told her aunt.

Her aunt reached out and placed a warm, reassuring hand on Roxie's arm. "I'm not judging you, child," she said softly. "I know that you did what you felt you had to do. But I know that you don't have any peace about it. That, I do know."

A sharp pain tore at Roxie's chest as she thought about Everett and how much her actions had hurt him.

"I should never have gotten married," Roxie confessed to her aunt. "I knew that it wasn't right."

Her aunt was silent for a few minutes. Then she asked, "Tell me. Do you love Everett?"

Roxie's answer was immediate. "I love him very much."

"So it wasn't a matter of not having love for the man, eh?" her aunt asked.

"No," Roxie admitted. "I'll love Everett till the day I die."

"Where there is love, I believe, there is always hope," Aunt Beryl commented, almost to herself.

"It's not that simple," Roxie replied. "I've done a terrible, terrible thing."

Aunt Beryl patted Roxie's arm. "You wouldn't be the first bride who bolted from her groom," she said.

"It's not that," said Roxie. "Although that was bad enough. What I've done is far worse . . . and irreversible."

"Irreversible?" Aunt Beryl asked. "What have you done that you can't undo?"

Roxie took a deep breath. It was time to unburden herself. She'd kept her secret for far too long. She knew Aunt Beryl wasn't the judgmental kind, but she also knew that what she said would hurt and would undoubtedly shock her favorite aunt.

As if she read Roxie's thoughts, Aunt Beryl squeezed Roxie's arm with gentle reassurance. "My love for you is unconditional, child," she said. "Nothing you say will ever change that. No matter what you've done or what you think you've done— you'll always have my support."

Roxie took another deep breath; then she told her aunt what she hadn't told anyone else—not her family, not her friends, not her husband.

"I'm pregnant," she said. "And I don't think that Everett is the father of the baby."

Chapter 11

Sinclair had forgotten the sound of Jamaica at night. When she'd visited the island as a child, she'd lie awake late at night and listen to the sound of crickets, seemingly thousands of them, as they sang away. She would also listen to the sound of rain. For her, this sound was familiar and comforting. This night was different. The sense of calm she'd felt when she'd landed on the island earlier had now disappeared; reality had intruded. After they'd arrived at her father's house in St. Christopher, Sinclair had called him. The news wasn't good. He still hadn't been able to get to Aunt Beryl's inn. The dirt roads that led through the Look Behind Mountains had been rendered impassable because of the sudden rains from a tropical storm approaching the island. Cassius had spoken to Roxie briefly by telephone, but she'd been too distraught to speak for long. When he'd tried to call her back, he'd discovered that the telephone landlines were down due to the storm, and there was no cell-phone service on that part of the island.

Her sister's mental state worried Sinclair. Her father had described her as seemingly on the brink of a nervous breakdown. She felt an urgency to be with Roxie, but her father had advised that they remain in St. Christopher until the storm passed, which would be at least another day. Everett had been upset by the news. He wanted to go to his wife quickly, and his plans were not working out. Everett, Ben, and Sinclair had shared a tense dinner at her father's home. Her father's cook, Dulcemina, had cooked a feast of curried chicken, rice and peas, plantains, and various other Jamaican dishes. Dulcemina was an excellent cook, but with the exception of Ben, no one had eaten much of her food. After dinner, Everett had excused himself and retired to his bedroom. After helping Dulcemina clear away and wash the dishes, Ben had gone upstairs to speak with Everett.

Night had fallen, and Sinclair walked over to the window seat in her father's living room. A reflection of Cassius's taste, the living room was filled with brightly colored Jamaican paintings and pictures of his family. The room was a perfect combination of charm and elegance, with its oversized pale beige couch; walnut, Victorian-inspired wingback chairs; and vases filled with native Jamaican flowers. It was a shame that it took family drama to bring Sinclair home to visit her father, she thought as she sat down on the window seat overlooking her father's garden. She'd been away from his home, and from him, for far too long.

Brutus, her father's ancient Great Dane, emerged

from another room and walked over to the window seat. Even at his advanced age, Brutus was still an imposing figure, causing fear in most who came to the house, although Sinclair knew that Brutus was more of a lover than a fighter. Her father had passed down his love of dogs, in particular, and of all other animals, to both of his daughters.

Sinclair leaned over and tickled Brutus behind his ears. "Hi, big daddy," she cooed. "I've missed you!"

A now-familiar, deep voice interrupted her playtime with Brutus. "I wish you'd be as welcoming to God's two-legged creatures as you are to his four-legged beasts."

Sinclair looked up to see Ben striding into the living room. He'd changed from his travel clothes, and he was now wearing jeans and a light blue T-shirt. Once again, in spite of everything that was going on, she felt a rush of attraction to him.

"I tend to find that God's four-legged creatures are a lot more trustworthy than his two-legged ones . . . particularly when the two legs in question belong to a man," Sinclair replied.

Ben sat next to her on the window seat. "To be so young, so beautiful, and so bitter," he said, with a wide smile. "It's a shame."

He was teasing her and this didn't sit well with Sinclair. She felt annoyed and she felt angry. How dare he make fun of her? Still, what was it about this man that made her angry and attracted to him at the same time? She wanted to scream at him, and she wanted to kiss him. It was the most unnerving and confusing sensation.

"What do you want?" Sinclair asked. "Did you come here to torment me?"

Ben leaned in closer. "Am I tormenting you, Sinclair?" he asked, his voice both low and seductive.

"Get thee behind me, Satan!" she wanted to yell at him, because he was surely the devil, or some relation, to make her want to do the things to him that were dancing in her head.

"It's a figure of speech," Sinclair replied, forcing her voice to remain calm.

He looked at her for a moment, as if he was deciding whether to ravish her mouth with kisses. Then he smiled and moved back just a little. Sinclair felt both disappointed and relieved—disappointed that she had been denied the pleasure of kissing him and relieved that he hadn't kissed her. With the strong attraction she felt to Ben, as well as her troubled emotional state, there was no telling what she'd end up doing with Ben—certainly something she'd regret in the clear light of morning.

"Any more word about your sister?" he asked, changing the subject.

Sinclair shook her head. "I tried calling both her and my dad, but they're having trouble with telephone lines. There's a bad storm approaching the island. That's why we're getting this rain."

"But your dad was able to get through earlier," Ben commented.

"Things have changed," Sinclair replied. "I'm sure we'll get phone service soon."

"What about the cell phone?" Ben asked.

"I can't get through on the cell, either," said Sinclair. "There's no cell-phone service where Roxie is staying, and when I call my dad's cell phone, I keep getting a fast busy signal. How's Everett?"

"Devastated," Ben replied.

Sinclair stood up. "Maybe I should go to him," she said.

Ben caught her hand. "Leave him alone," he said gently. "He's not up to company right now."

Sinclair sat down again, but Ben still held her hand. It was strange, but despite her turmoil about her feelings for him, she felt comfortable holding his hand. It was as if her hands belonged in his. Just then, Brutus started barking at Ben.

"He wants you to pet him," Sinclair explained.

"Do you speak, Great Dane?" Ben teased.

Sinclair ignored the jibe. "Go ahead and pet him. He wants to get to know you better."

"He should know me well enough," Ben commented. "He was humping my leg all through dinner."

Sinclair burst into laughter. Even in this crazy time, Ben was able to make her laugh. It felt good to feel a rush of amusement, even if it was only momentary.

"Why didn't you stop him?" she asked, when her laughter subsided.

"Hell, he probably weighs more than I do. I'm not trying to pick a fight with him."

"He probably knows you're easy." Sinclair smiled. "He didn't hump my leg."

He looked at her again. "You should smile more," he said.

"And you should pet Brutus."

"I don't like dogs."

"How could you not like dogs?"

"It's easy. One of them bit me on my seventh birthday. Since then, I've done my best to avoid them."

He was still holding her hand. As she looked

into Ben's eyes, Sinclair thought she saw a questioning look in his eyes, as if he was trying to figure her out. Suddenly, she knew she was going to get a kiss.

He leaned in closer.

"My sister has run away," she murmured.

"Yes," he replied. "That's true."

He moved even closer.

"And the man she left behind, your best friend, is devastated and upstairs."

"That is also true," Ben replied, moving closer still.

"You're too good-looking, and you fear commitment," Sinclair whispered.

"Guilty as charged."

His lips were almost touching hers.

"Also, you don't like dogs," said Sinclair, right before his lips crashed down on hers. She felt herself fall into a heady abyss, as Sinclair gave into her feelings. As he kissed her, Brutus barked. It was clear that Brutus disapproved. Sinclair knew that if she had any sense, she'd heed Brutus' warnings, and run like the very devil himself was chasing her. But she was powerless to stop his kiss just as she was powerless to stop herself from kissing him back. *Lord knows, I'll regret this in the morning,* was Sinclair's last coherent thought as she felt Ben's fingers unbutton her blouse.

Ben held on tight as he carried Sinclair upstairs. Outside, he could hear the heavy rains from the tropical storm lash against the windows. The storm outside was fierce, but it was nothing compared to the storm that was raging inside him. His need for

Sinclair could best be described as desperate. He
wanted her body. That was clear. But what frightened him to the core was his desire for more than
her body. He wanted *her*—her dreams, her fears,
her very soul. He felt connected to this woman,
and he knew, even as the desire to possess her intimately held him in a viselike grip, that he was not
going to let Sinclair Dearheart exit his life.

He knew she was feeling the exact feelings that
tore at him. As he carried her upstairs, he felt her
heart pounding. When he reached his bedroom
upstairs, he gently lowered her on the bed. Her
eyes were closed. She was scared. He knew that
she'd been hurt, and as he watched her lying on
his bed, he felt a strong wave of possessiveness,
which rocked him. He would never let anyone else
hurt this woman, *his woman*.

"Open your eyes," he softly commanded as he
lay down next to her. She obeyed his command,
and the hunger he saw in her eyes, the hunger for
him, was almost his undoing.

Her shirt was open, revealing a pink lace bra,
which he intended to take off with all deliberate
speed.

"I'm not sure that this is a very good idea," she
said. He could hear the slight tremor in her voice,
confirming her fear.

He leaned over and gave her a light kiss. "It's
a very, very good idea," he murmured against
her lips.

He heard her soft moan, and any self-control he
possessed was shattered in that moment. He deepened his kiss, ravishing her mouth, tasting her
tongue, her lips, her cheek, her eyelids. He show-

ered her with kisses as she whispered the word *please* over and over again.

He pulled back for a moment and stared at her. She was a beautiful woman, and the desire she felt for him only amplified her beauty.

"Are you scared?" he asked her as she stared back at him.

"Yes," she replied.

"What are you scared of?" he asked.

She gave him a wry smile. "I'm scared of us."

"I'm glad you understand that there is an *us*," Ben replied, his voice hoarse with desire.

He watched as she shook her head in frustration. He could see her desire, and he could see her fear. Both emotions were waging war inside her.

"Let it go, baby," he whispered to her as he caressed her face. "Let it all go. The fear, the disappointment, the anger. Let it all go."

"I don't know if I can," she answered.

"Then," he said as he lowered himself to the bed, pulling her close to him, "let me show you how."

This time he kissed her mouth slowly, gently, giving her time to catch up with him. It didn't take long. She raised her hands and placed them at the sides of his face, deepening the kiss. Ben needed no more urging.

He tore away from her mouth, and his lips found her sexy pink bra. Pushing the cups of the garment away, he kissed one nipple, then the other, her soft moans urging him on, but he decided to take his time with this particular feast. He could feel her heart hammering as he continued this intimate kiss, or was it his heart that was hammering against his chest? He couldn't tell.

"Ben," she called out.

He paused and looked up at her. "What is it, baby?"

"I want . . ." Her breath was coming in soft, ragged gasps. "I want . . ."

"What do you want, Sinclair?" he asked. "Tell me."

Her eyes told him what her lips couldn't, and he complied with her request as he lowered his mouth and began a trail of slow kisses that went from her breast, down to her navel, and then down below.

"No!" she cried out as he began the most intimate of kisses.

He pulled away for a minute, then gave her a wicked grin. "Yes."

When he continued his intimate kiss, he could feel her nails raking across his back.

"Yes," she said softly. Then she called out again, louder now, "Yes!"

He could feel her trembling beneath his lips. She was moaning now, loudly. *Good,* he thought, with perverse pleasure. He'd never liked it when women were quiet in bed. He wanted to hear their pleasure, and he could both hear and feel as the pleasure surged and shattered in Sinclair.

Afterwards, he left the bed and walked over to his overnight bag. Opening it, he found the box of condoms he'd purchased before the trip. He'd known that there was no way he was going to be in close proximity to Sinclair without making love to her. The last time he hadn't been prepared. He wasn't about to make the same mistake twice.

He put on a condom and walked back over to the bed.

Sinclair smiled at him.

"Round two?" she asked mischievously.

"Oh yeah," he replied as he got back into bed. Pulling her on top of him, he entered her, and his senses exploded. He watched as her eyes widened as the pleasure she felt ignited. He grabbed her hips as she began moving, slowly at first.

He gritted his teeth as he felt the heat inside him grow with each slow movement. Then, her rhythm quickened, and he held on, the sweet pressure inside him rising as he matched her rhythm, thrust for thrust. Just as he felt himself about to slide off the precipice, he watched as Sinclair threw her head back, engulfed in another climax, and then he joined her in an earthshaking, gravity-defying, head-spinning, almost religious experience.

Chapter 12

Ben awoke the next morning to the very loud snoring of Brutus, the Great Dane, who had somehow managed to get himself into Ben's bed. Looking around the room, he could see that Sinclair was nowhere to be found. *What is it with these Dearheart women? They are always running away,* he thought as he stretched out in bed, trying not to wake or in any other way annoy the sleeping Brutus. Glancing at the clock on the wall, he saw that it was just past eight o'clock, which was late for him. Ben was used to being an early riser, but the delectable Sinclair had worn him out last night. Thoughts of the night he and Sinclair had shared brought a fresh wave of desire to him. Their lovemaking had lasted until the early-morning hours, when they'd both fallen into an exhausted sleep.

Brutus raised his head and looked at him, as if to say, "What the hell are you doing in my bed?"

Dogs had always made him uncomfortable, and Brutus was no exception. People who were animal lovers mystified him. It wasn't as if he hated four-legged creatures; he just believed in giving them a wide berth. The dog bite he'd received as a child only increased his initial fear that animals in general, and dogs in particular, didn't like him. He was the kind of person that dogs barked at angrily while ignoring all others around him.

"Are you going to start barking at me, too?" he asked Brutus as he carefully sat up. "And when did you get here?"

Brutus looked at him with contempt, but to the Great Dane's credit, he didn't bark, although he let out a low growl. Sinclair had assured him that Brutus was a pussycat, but at a hundred twenty pounds, give or take a few, Brutus looked more like a horse than a dog, and an angry horse at that.

The door to his bedroom opened, and Sinclair walked in, looking more sexy and beautiful than anyone had a right to be at eight o'clock in the morning. She was dressed in a bright yellow sundress with spaghetti straps that showed off her beautiful shoulders to her advantage. He longed to kiss at least one of those brown shoulders. Once again, the passion he felt for her flared up, and he fought the urge to grab her and throw her on the bed.

"Hey, beautiful," he said, smiling at her. "Why'd you leave me in bed with Killer here?"

Sinclair walked over to where Ben was sitting and stood before him.

"You're more dangerous than Brutus," she replied. "He's a pussycat."

Ben wrapped his hands around Sinclair's waist

and pulled her close to him. She felt warm and safe. She felt like she was coming home.

"I wouldn't exactly call me dangerous," Ben said. "I would call me—"

"Horny?" Sinclair interjected.

Ben pulled her down on his lap and nuzzled her neck. "Something like that," he murmured. "Only I wouldn't put it in such crass terms."

He heard her sharp intake of breath as he started nibbling on her shoulder blade.

"Stop," she said, although to him, she didn't sound convincing.

"You want me to stop?" he asked softly in between feasting on her shoulders and her neck.

"Yes." She breathed out the word. "Please."

He increased the pressure and began exploring other delectable parts of Sinclair with his hands.

"Ben, we need to focus here," Sinclair said, but her voice trembled. "We're here to get Roxie."

"No reason why we can't have fun doing that," Ben responded.

Sinclair wiggled out of his grasp. "Yes, there is," she replied. "We need to plan our day. I got through to Dad on the telephone, and he thinks that he'll be able to get to Roxie today. But it's going to be tough going because even though the rains have stopped, the roads are still pretty muddy, and there's been word of overturned trees and mud slides. Dad wants us to wait here. He plans on bringing Roxie back. But I want to stick to the original plan and meet Dad at Aunt Beryl's place."

"Your dad's plan sounds more practical," Ben replied.

"You've traveled all over the world for your stories," said Sinclair indignantly. "From what Roxie and Everett said, you've been in some dangerous places and in some tough situations. Nothing stopped you. Why should anything stop me from going to my sister?"

"Common sense?" Ben asked. "I mean, it's not that overrated, Sinclair."

That look of stubborn determination, which Ben now recognized and, in spite of himself, admired, crossed Sinclair's face.

"Roxie's my sister. I don't expect you to tag along. You can wait here. I'm sure Everett still wants to go with me, but even if he doesn't, I've already made arrangements to drive to Port Antonio this afternoon. I'll stay there tonight. Then tomorrow morning, I'll go on to Aunt Beryl's inn."

"Do you think I'd let you run around Jamaica by yourself?" Ben asked.

"You'd *let* me?" Sinclair asked, bristling at his choice of words. "The last time I checked, I didn't need your permission for anything. You're good in bed, but not good enough for me to take orders from you."

Instead of being offended by her sharp words, Ben found himself getting turned on. "I used a poor choice of words," he said, trying to mollify her. "What I meant to say is that it would be difficult for me if you went away without me. I'd miss you. Who would protect me from this beast you call a dog if you went away?"

She narrowed her eyes speculatively, as if she wasn't quite sure whether or not to believe him. Then, she said, "I'm planning to leave sometime midmorning."

"Then I guess that's the time that I'll be leaving, too," said Ben.

Sinclair stood up. "Breakfast is ready downstairs in the dining room."

Once again, Ben pulled her back on his lap. "You know," he said in between light kisses, "I'm not really that hungry."

Sinclair sighed as she returned the kisses. "Neither am I."

Brutus began barking, but Ben wasn't listening, and he suspected, from the moans that were coming from Sinclair, that she wasn't listening to Brutus, either.

"Where to, boss?" The cabdriver seemed impatient and wanted to be on his way.

"I'm going to a place called Blue Horizons Inn," said Everett. "It's in a village called Pemberley, in Portland Parish."

The cabdriver turned on the ignition. "Yeah, mon, I know the place. It's out by the mountains. It's far from here, you know?"

Everett leaned back in his seat. "So I've heard," he said.

"I mean, it's clear across the island. The roads are pretty bad. It's going to cost you a lot of money for me to take you there, mon."

Everett fought hard to keep the impatience out of his voice. "I don't care how much it costs. Just get me there."

"Respect," said the cabdriver. "I didn't mean no harm. It's just that I didn't want you to be surprised when it comes time to pay up, you know?"

For a fleeting moment, Everett wondered if he should have waited for Ben and Sinclair, but he'd awakened this morning with a firm resolve to find Roxie. He wanted to see her as soon as possible, and he wanted to be alone when he saw her. He knew that her father would probably be there at the inn with Roxie and her aunt, but he suspected that both Cassius and Beryl would give them space. Although he loved Sinclair, he knew that her close bond with her sister would compel her to stay by her side.

Driving into St. Christopher yesterday, he'd seen a taxi stand by the marketplace. It was a walk of less than a mile from Cassius's home to the marketplace, and Everett had left the house quietly before anyone was awake. He'd thought that the cook might have seen him, but he wasn't sure. He'd left in a hurry, with just the clothes on his back and a small duffel bag with a single change of clothing and a toothbrush. He'd get whatever else he needed when he got to Pemberley.

"How long will it take us to get to Pemberley?" Everett asked as the cab made its way through the already-crowded streets of St. Christopher.

"Couldn't really say," the cabdriver responded. "Typically, it's about five or six hours, but with the rains yesterday making a mess of these roads, it could be an all-day affair. Best settle in and enjoy the scenery. I tell you the truth, mon. There's no place as beautiful as Jamaica, so you might as well enjoy the sights."

Everett suppressed a sigh. As undeniably beautiful as the island was, the only thing on his mind was finding Roxie and convincing her to come back home with him.

Chapter 13

It wasn't until after breakfast that Sinclair discovered that Everett was gone. At first she hadn't been alarmed when she'd knocked on the door and no one answered. The cook had informed her that Everett had taken a walk earlier that morning, and even though Everett had already been gone for a few hours, Sinclair assumed that he had a lot on his mind, and she was sure that the walk was a form of therapy for Everett. Still, she wondered why he would stay away so long when he'd been so anxious to find Roxie.

When, at almost eleven o'clock, Ben went into Everett's room to find some aftershave lotion in Everett's duffel bag, he realized that both the duffel bag and Everett were gone. Ben went back to the kitchen, where Sinclair and the cook were having a conversation about Jamaican politics.

"Was Everett carrying a bag with him when he left?" Ben asked the cook, Dulcemina, who nodded in the affirmative.

"Why would he need a bag if he was just going

for a walk?" Sinclair asked, knowing the answer even before she finished the question.

"I thought the same thing, too," said Dulcemina, "but I didn't pay it too much mind, because the poor thing must be going out of his head with worry."

"He's gone to find Roxie," Ben said grimly. "Without us."

"That doesn't make any sense," said Sinclair. "Why didn't he wait for us?"

"I guess maybe you two were busy," said Dulcemina blandly, but Sinclair could see that there was a teasing sparkle in her eye. Did the whole house know what she'd been up to?

Ben cleared his throat. "We need to go after him. In the state he's in, he's not thinking clearly."

Sinclair's mind raced. Everett had a good two-to three-hour head start on them. "We'll never catch him."

"What about his cell phone?" Ben asked.

"He was complaining about that yesterday," Dulcemina commented. "He said his cell phone didn't work down here."

"I doubt he'd even answer it, even if it did work," said Ben.

At that moment, the telephone started ringing.

"Maybe it's Everett," Sinclair said hopefully as she reached for the telephone receiver. "Hello."

It was her father.

"I'm getting ready to leave for Pemberley," her father said. He sounded tired.

"Everett's gone," said Sinclair. "We think that he's on his way to see Roxie."

Her father let out a long sigh. "I can't say that I

blame him," said Cassius. "I would probably have done the same thing."

No, you wouldn't, Sinclair thought. You would let Roxie go, just like you let Mom go, just like you let Roxie and me go. Sinclair loved her father, but her father's refusal to fight for his family still hurt. When he moved back to Jamaica, Sinclair had felt that he'd run away from her and from Roxie. She understood her father's need to get away from her mother: their animosity toward each other was legendary. But Sinclair could never understand how he'd walked away from his daughters. She pushed those thoughts out of her head. She needed to focus on the here and now.

"Dad, we're leaving for Pemberley soon," said Sinclair.

"Okay," her father replied. "Cordis will drive you there."

"Thanks, Dad. When you see Roxie, tell her that I love her."

Her father sighed again. "I'll do that. I spoke to Beryl, and she said that your sister wasn't doing too well."

Feelings of guilt gripped her. While she was getting her groove on, Roxie was going through an emotional crisis. What kind of sister was she? Hell, what kind of human being was she? She shot Ben a dark glare. After all, it was *his* fault that she'd gotten distracted. She told her father, "I'll be there as soon as possible."

After she ended her telephone conversation with her father, Sinclair walked out of the kitchen and into the dining room, with Ben following close behind.

Turning to face him, she said, "Maybe I should go to Pemberley alone."

Dark eyebrows shot up. "Come again?"

Noting Ben's glowering expression, Sinclair pushed her shoulders back, took a deep breath, and said, "I think you should stay here."

"I thought that's what you said. What's this about? An hour ago we were making love, and now you're telling me to stay here while you leave? That won't happen."

"That's just the point," said Sinclair, letting free her exasperation. "The whole making love part. It's inappropriate . . . especially with everything my sister's going through. I can't afford to be distracted now."

Ben narrowed his eyes. "Your sister is a grown woman. She made certain choices, and you can't feel bad if she can't handle the consequences of those choices."

Anger flared between them. "You don't know anything about my sister."

"I know that she got married one day, and the very next day she left her husband, without having the guts to tell him to his face."

What he said was true, but she would be damned if she let anyone talk about her sister, even if what they were saying was 100 percent accurate.

"I can't explain her actions, because I haven't talked to her, but I know that she had a good reason for her actions. She isn't a cruel person. She wouldn't hurt Everett if there wasn't something else going on."

"Something other than her lack of integrity, you mean?"

Sinclair spun around. "I'm going alone," she said.

Ben took two strides, and then he pulled her back firmly in his arms.

Turning to face him, Sinclair said, "Let me go!" She was angry, hurt, and still very attracted to this maddening man. "Leave me alone."

"Not until you understand that I'm going with you."

"Why would you want to go? You don't care about Roxie," said Sinclair.

"I care about Everett," said Ben as he released her from his grip. "And I care about you."

"You care about me?"

"Yes. I care about you. Very much."

"The last man that said those words walked out on me on our wedding anniversary to go live with a woman who'd had a boob job."

Ben swore under his breath. "He was a fool. I'm not."

Sinclair shook her head. "It doesn't matter. I need to get to my sister."

"And I need to get to my friend."

Seeing the look of grim determination in Ben's eyes, Sinclair knew that she wasn't going to win this battle. Still, she didn't have to be gracious about it. "Fine," she said. "Be ready in five minutes."

"I'll be ready in three," he replied.

Just before she walked out the dining-room door, he called her name. She turned to look at him.

"Don't think about leaving without me," said Ben. "I'll find you."

"Is that some sort of threat?" Sinclair asked, bristling at his he-man act.

"No," Ben said, with a maddeningly sexy smile. "It's a promise."

* * *

Everett reached the inn just after sundown. It had been a long, and at times tedious, trip, but he was finally at Blue Horizons Inn. After paying the cabdriver his fare and a generous tip, he exited the vehicle and walked up the narrow cobblestone path that led to the front veranda of the inn. He walked up to the front door and opened it. He was greeted by the smell of Jamaican cooking and a tall, thin woman who looked like Cassius and who was sitting behind an antique mahogany desk in the small lobby area, just off a large living room.

She smiled at him, and he could see the compassion in her eyes.

"You must be Everett," she said in her soft Jamaican lilt. "We've been expecting you."

Dispensing with all formality, Everett asked, "Where is Roxie?"

"I'm right here, Everett."

Everett turned to see his wife walking slowly down the stairs, with her father following close behind. She looked tired, and her face looked as if she'd been crying. She was dressed in a tie-dyed Bob Marley T-shirt and some cutoff denim shorts that were too large for her. Her feet were bare.

"Hello, Everett," said Cassius Dearheart. He greeted his son-in-law with a firm handshake.

"Hello, sir," Everett replied, keeping his eyes fixed on Roxie. After everything she'd put him through these last few days, one thing was certain. He still loved her.

Roxie turned to her father and said, "I think

Everett and I have some things to say to each other in private."

Cassius looked anxious at his daughter's words, but he nodded his head. "I'm here if you need me," he said, his voice gruff.

Roxie walked out of the living room and onto the veranda. Everett followed her. He watched as she sat down on one of the white wicker rocking chairs, and then he sat on another chair, beside his wife.

"What's going on, Roxie?" Everett asked his new wife. "Did I do something? Did I hurt you? What did I do?"

"You didn't do anything," Roxie replied, her voice shaking.

"Then did someone else—"

"I did this to myself," said Roxie. "No one did this to me. This is my fault."

"Whatever it is, why didn't you talk to me about it? I woke up after our wedding night, and you were gone."

"I know you're angry with me," Roxie said, her voice still shaking. She wouldn't look at him.

"I'm more confused than angry," Everett replied. "Will you tell me what's going on?"

He watched as Roxie began to wring her hands in her lap as she stared down at the floor.

"This is bad, isn't it?" Everett asked.

Roxie nodded her head. Large teardrops fell from her eyes and rolled down her cheeks. "It's unforgivable."

Everett digested the words in silence.

Finally, Roxie turned and faced him. "First, I need to tell you that I love you. I will always love you."

Everett let her continue talking even as he tried to prepare himself for what was obviously going to be very bad news.

"A few months ago, I did something horrible. I slept with my ex-boyfriend Phillip . . . I don't know why I did it. A part of me wanted to see if I still had feelings for him . . . I don't . . . and a part of me was scared about what I felt . . . what I feel for you . . . I don't know why I did it."

Everett was not a violent man, and the feeling of white hot rage that gripped him scared him. He was a man who'd always prided himself on having control, but he felt as if something had gripped him and was tearing him apart. The pain he felt was indescribable. It was as if someone with an iron fist had punched him squarely in the gut.

"That's not all . . . ," Roxie continued.

"There's more?" Everett asked in disbelief.

Roxie nodded her head. "I'm so sorry," she whispered. "I'm going to have a baby . . ."

"And you think the baby is his?" Everett asked.

"I don't know. I think so."

Everett felt a roaring in his ears. At first, it had been a dull noise rushing all around him, but then it grew into a roar, threatening to consume him. The woman he loved and married had cheated on him. And she was going to have a baby. A baby that might not be his.

"If you didn't love me, why didn't you just tell me?" he asked, his hoarse voice betraying his pain.

She reached over and touched his arm, and Everett flinched as if he were in pain.

"Is it still going on?" he asked. "This thing with your ex?"

"No," she said. "It was only one night."

"I don't believe you," said Everett. He was taught that men didn't cry. He was taught that men were always to be in control of their emotions. He was taught to be strong in all situations. But as he felt his world crumble around him, he felt the tears falling down his face. The last time he'd cried was when his grandmother died.

"It's true," Roxie said as she started to cry also.

Everett refused to let his heart soften. Wiping away his tears with an angry hand, he asked, "Does he know about the baby?"

"I told him," Roxie said in between her sobs. "He doesn't want anything to do with the baby or with me."

Everett stood up. "When the baby's born, you're going to take a blood test." Jamming his fists into the pockets of his jacket, he added, "If the baby is mine, I'm going to be a part of his life."

The roaring in his ears reached a crescendo.

Chapter 14

"Wake up, sleeping beauty."

Sinclair awoke from a dream-filled sleep to find that they'd finally reached her aunt's inn. Someone was gently shaking her. It was Ben.

"Were you dreaming about me?" he asked her softly.

"Surprisingly, no," Sinclair said, annoyed. Even though what had occurred last night and this morning had probably increased Ben's already large ego, his flirting, particularly with everything going on, was horribly timed. Still, the warm feeling in the pit of her stomach when he was near annoyed her even more.

The journey to Pemberley had been exhausting. Long delays, bad roads made worse by the rains, and the presence of Ben Easington had made for an uncomfortable ride. At some point between the towns of Ocho Rios and Port Antonio, she'd fallen asleep. Night had fallen, and the well-lit inn nestled in the dramatic Look Behind Mountains looked cozy and inviting. This was the perfect place for her intensely private and eccentric aunt.

"I'll help Cordis with the bags," said Ben. "Go in to your sister."

When Sinclair entered the inn, she saw that her father was sitting on one of the three couches in the living room. There was another couple sitting in the corner, sipping wine and talking. Turning her attention back to her father, she saw that he looked tired and old. A feeling of fear gripped her. She realized that both her parents were getting older, and the thought that one day she would be here without them frightened her. Her family was dysfunctional, and sometimes plain old crazy, but despite her parents' rocky relationship, she knew that they would both be there to support her in times of crisis. Her father was there for Roxie, and he had been there for Sinclair during her divorce. Even her mother, who was prone to hysteria on occasion, would comfort her when life got too overwhelming. *I need to call them both more,* she vowed.

Her father looked up as she approached him.

"Hi, Daddy," said Sinclair as she sat next to him on the couch. It had been years since she'd called him that, but the word came naturally to her today.

The smile on her father's face when he first saw her warmed Sinclair's heart.

"Hi, sweetheart. I'm glad you're here."

"What's going on?"

Her father shook his head. "It isn't good," he said.

"Do you know what's going on?" Sinclair asked her father.

"I do," he replied. "But I'll let Roxie talk to you about it. It's her story to tell."

"How is she?" Sinclair asked. "Did Everett get here yet?"

"She's not doing too good," he replied. "And Everett's not doing too much better. He got here a couple of hours ago. They talked. He's upset. She's upset. I tried to talk to Everett, but he was in no mood for a discussion."

"His friend Ben is here with me. I'm sure he'll be able to reach Everett."

Her father looked at her, his expression unreadable. "He sounds like a good man to be so loyal to his friend."

Sinclair didn't respond. Ben was a good man. She couldn't imagine Wayne doing the same for anyone. Her ex-husband always put his own needs first, and if he did something kind, there was usually a benefit for him in the act of kindness. Looking back, Sinclair knew that there had to be some good qualities about Wayne, but for the life of her, other than his elegant wardrobe and good conversation, she was drawing a blank.

"Go to your sister," her father said. "She needs you."

"Where is she?" Sinclair asked.

"She's sitting in the garden . . . It's in the back."

Sinclair found her sister sitting in the dark in her aunt's garden. Sinclair sat beside her on the wrought-iron bench and held her sister's hand. She could hear the loud symphony of crickets and the insistent calls of night birds.

Roxie looked at her, and Sinclair could see the anguish in her eyes.

Sinclair said the first thing that came to her mind. "It's going to be all right."

Roxie shook her head. "It's never going to be all right again."

Sinclair squeezed her hand. "Talk to me, Roxie. What's going on?"

"I'm pregnant."

Sinclair wasn't sure what she'd expected to hear, but she hadn't expected to hear *that*. She'd thought that Roxie would tell her that maybe she'd fallen in love with another man, or maybe she'd fallen out of love with Everett, and that she'd just gone through with the wedding to save face.

"Roxie, that's wonderful news," Sinclair said.

"I'm not sure that Everett is the father."

Sinclair digested this information.

"That's not so wonderful," Sinclair finally said. "But, honey, it's not the end of the world."

"The baby might be Phillip's."

Sinclair felt her heart drop to the pit of her stomach. The family had cried out a collective hallelujah when Roxie finally dumped her crazy ex-boyfriend Phillip. "A Harvard-educated con artist," was the description her father had given Phillip, and it had been an appropriate description. He was always coming up with some get-rich-quick scheme that invariably left him close to bankruptcy. He was unscrupulous, and he was charming. Phillip had been Roxie's college sweetheart, but no one could understand the attraction. He was good-looking, but he was loud and crass. He had also been insanely jealous of any man who even looked at Roxie, and he had tried to keep Roxie away from the family. They'd broken up countless times, and each time Phillip would convince Roxie to give him another chance. Roxie had finally gotten off that toxic merry-go-round and gave him the boot, but it took a while.

Roxie's voice trembled when she spoke. "I betrayed Everett, Sinclair. I betrayed him and destroyed him."

"Folks find their way back from cheating," Sinclair said, putting her arms around Roxie's shoulders. "I did."

Roxie turned and looked at her. "Did you?" she asked. "Did you ever get over what Wayne did to you?"

"I can't tell you that after all this time, it doesn't hurt when I think about what he did," Sinclair replied honestly. "But I've moved on with my life. Everett will, too."

"You should have seen the way he looked at me," Roxie continued. "I think he hates me."

"He's hurt," said Sinclair. "And I'm sure he's angry. But Everett doesn't hate you. He's not the kind to carry hate in his heart."

Roxie started to cry, and Sinclair held her sister in her arms. Stroking Roxie's back, she let her sister pour out her pain. From the time she'd first held her sister as a little baby, she'd vowed that she would always be there for Roxie. She'd been there when bullies pushed her sister down in the playground. She'd been there when Roxie had her first broken heart. She'd been there when Roxie went through her wild times in college. She'd been there for her sister every time she'd called, and she wasn't going to turn her back on Roxie now, even though what she'd done to Everett was horrible.

Sinclair knew firsthand the kind of pain cheating inflicted on the one who'd trusted and been betrayed. She remembered the agony—there was no other word—of finding out that the world that she'd so carefully crafted was false. With cheating came lies, deception. It was a long road back to trusting again, and Sinclair wasn't sure she could ever trust another man after what Wayne had done to her. Not only did Everett have to live with the fact that his wife had been unfaithful to him, he had to deal with the baby. The baby was innocent, but Sinclair knew that this child would be a reminder of Roxie's unfaithfulness. How does one get back from that, she wondered?

"Whatever you decide," said Sinclair, "I'm going to support you. You're not going through this alone."

"I'm going to keep my baby," Roxie said when she stopped crying.

"And I'm going to support you," Sinclair repeated.

"I'm scared," Roxie whispered.

"I know," said Sinclair. "But we'll figure this out together."

"Sinclair, can you talk to Everett? He's in so much pain."

"I'll talk to him, but right now he probably needs a whole lot of space."

"I should have told him before the wedding . . . I tried the time I asked you to get him . . . right before the wedding," Roxie said. "I told him that I had something he needed to know, and he told me that all he wanted to know was whether I loved him."

"Do you still want Everett in your life?" Sinclair asked.

"Yes," said Roxie.

"Then why'd you run away, baby?"

"I was scared. I didn't want him to know the truth about me. I didn't want him to look at me the way he looked at me today."

"Why didn't you talk to me?"

"Sinclair, I couldn't. You've always been Miss Perfect, and I've always been Miss-Prone-to-Getting-Her-Behind-in-Trouble."

Sinclair shook her head in amazement. "Is that how you see me? As being perfect? I'm hardly perfect, Roxie. I've been hiding from life for the past two years."

"Yeah, but you're strong. You kept on working. You kept on living. You didn't miss a beat."

"I cried myself to sleep every night for over a year, and I'm still seeing a therapist," Sinclair replied. "You're a strong woman, stronger than you give yourself credit for."

"Well, I'm going to have to be strong. I'm going to be a mother in six months."

Chapter 15

Sinclair sat on the chair in her sister's bedroom and watched her sleep. They'd talked for several hours in the garden, and it had been close to midnight when Sinclair had finally convinced Roxie to go upstairs to her room. Sinclair had remained in Roxie's room even after Roxie had fallen asleep. Sinclair sat in the quiet room, playing Roxie's words over in her head. *I'm going to be a mother, Sinclair.* It was hard picturing her baby sister, with her well-known streak of irresponsibility, as a mother. Especially under these hard circumstances. Roxie had always wanted children, and she and Everett had both decided on a big family, but now that dream had gone awry. Still, there was joy in the fact that a little baby would be joining the family in a few months. Sinclair was going to be an aunt.

Sinclair had tried to convey the positive aspects of this drama to her sister, but fear was Roxie's overriding emotion when it came to the prospect of childbirth. Roxie was afraid of how her child would be accepted by the rest of the family. She knew her

mother was going to freak out. And even though
the rest of the family wasn't as uptight as Belinda
Rose, there was bound to be talk—ugly talk—about
the circumstances under which this child was con-
ceived. "In terms of family scandal, this is definitely
worse than our great-grandmother's nude por-
traits," Roxie had wailed. True enough, there were
many in their family who would judge Roxie harshly
for her actions, but Sinclair was certain that as dysfunctional and dramatic as her family was, folks
would eventually rally around Roxie and her baby.

"Everyone loves babies," Sinclair had reasoned.
"The family will soon be fighting over baby-sitting
rights."

"Mom doesn't love babies," Roxie had replied
darkly. "And she's especially not going to love my
fatherless baby."

"Your baby isn't fatherless," Sinclair had replied.
"He's got a father."

"Yes, that's true," Roxie had wailed. "I just don't
know who the father is."

Sinclair had hugged her sister tight. "Your baby
is going to be fine, and so are you."

In her heart, Sinclair knew that this was true, but
she also knew that this was a tough situation—
tough for Roxie, and tougher for Everett. Sinclair
knew firsthand the pain of a cheating partner, but
a cheating partner with a baby as the end result—
that was exponentially harder. Her heart went out
to Everett. She'd tried to leave Roxie periodically
through the evening to talk to her brother-in-law,
but Roxie had clung to her.

"Don't leave me," Roxie had begged, and Sinclair
had complied with that request. As much as she

wanted to make sure that Everett was doing the best he could under the circumstances, she couldn't leave her sister. The panic and the fear that Sinclair saw in Roxie's eyes kept her by her sister's side. She knew in her heart that Ben would be there for Everett, just as she was there for her sister.

Both her father and her aunt had come by at various times to see if Roxie needed them, but they'd given Sinclair a wide berth to console her sister. The family knew that the bond between the two sisters was strong, and Cassius and Beryl respected that bond, unlike their mother, who would have barged in and made her presence, and her disapproval, felt. At the thought of her mother, Sinclair cringed. She knew that her father had spoken with her mother about the true nature of Roxie's drama. Sinclair had asked her father how her mother had reacted to the news. She knew that Cassius's terse reply that their mother had not taken this particular bit of news well was probably the understatement of the year. She could only imagine the state of hysteria that her mother had undoubtedly worked herself into at this point.

Sinclair leaned over and stroked her sister's forehead. When they were children, Roxie would ask Sinclair to stay with her in Roxie's bedroom until she fell asleep. Roxie had been convinced that there were ghosts hiding under her bed, and only the presence of Sinclair would keep the ghosts from devouring her. Sinclair would joke that she was there to chase the ghosts away. Just as she had when they were children, Sinclair stayed in Roxie's room to chase the ghosts away—ghosts of fear and ghosts of disappointment.

"It's going to be okay," Sinclair whispered in her sleeping sister's ear. "It's going to be okay. You and the baby are going to be fine."

Once again, Sinclair's mind turned to Everett. It was obvious that despite everything that had happened, Roxie still loved her husband. She'd talked about him constantly—alternately despairing that she'd hurt him and worrying that he'd never forgive her.

"Give him time to come to terms with everything," Sinclair had advised her sister. But despite her supportive words, Sinclair knew in her heart that sometimes there wasn't that much forgiveness in the world. She'd walked away and never looked back under similar circumstances. She couldn't blame Everett if he felt the same way.

The clock on the wall informed her that it was now well past midnight. It was time for Sinclair to go to bed. Although she was tired, Sinclair knew there were too many things running around her head for her to sleep. She stood up, turned out the light, and walked out of Roxie's room. Bypassing her own room, Sinclair walked down the stairs, past the lobby, and into the small library she'd noticed when she first arrived. She wanted to be alone, but she didn't want to be in her room. She hoped that her aunt's well-stocked library contained some reading material that would take her attention away from more pressing matters or something that would make her sleepy. The library was dark, but she could see the outline of someone very familiar by the window. Ben was sitting on the windowsill. Startled, Sinclair let out a small scream.

"I'd love to make you scream," he said, "but not this way. I can think of more pleasurable ways of—"

Sinclair cut him off. She was in no mood for flirting. "Well, what do you expect?" she asked, annoyed that she'd let him startle her, and annoyed that he'd had the bad manners to remind her of their very recent indiscretion. "What sane person sits in the dark? Why aren't you in bed, anyway?"

"I could ask you the same question," Ben replied.

"I can't sleep," said Sinclair. She sighed and turned on one of the lamps in the library, flooding the room with a soft, warm glow. Ben looked tired. He was obviously feeling the strain that she was feeling.

Ben stood up and walked over to her. "You can't sleep. I can't sleep. I can think of a way to relieve a little of the tension you're feeling."

Sinclair took a step back. "I bet you can," she said darkly.

She watched as he grinned back at her. "Get your mind out of the gutter," he said. "I wasn't suggesting that we make love to each other, although that wouldn't be a bad idea."

"It would be a bad idea," Sinclair snapped. "A bad idea in very poor taste."

He pulled her into his arms, and despite her protest, she felt a warm flush in the base of her stomach. He leaned down and spoke softly in her ear. "Let me give you one of my world-changing massages."

She stiffened. "No thank you."

He pulled her closer, and Sinclair was acutely aware of how well their bodies fit together.

"Why do you fight me on everything, woman?" Ben asked, his voice still gentle. He had moved his hands to her shoulders, and he began slowly massaging them.

"I don't fight you on everything," Sinclair replied, trying not to focus on how heavenly his hands felt as he slowly kneaded the tight muscles in her shoulders and upper arms. It felt heavenly.

"Yes, you do," he whispered. "Actually, it turns me on."

"You're a pervert," Sinclair replied as she felt the tension of the day wear away. "Who taught you to do this, anyway?" she asked. "Did you date a masseuse?"

She was rewarded by a deep chuckle. "What a sexist remark, Ms. Dearheart. I expect better from you. The truth is, this is something that I picked up a while ago."

"Another tool of seduction?" Sinclair murmured as visions of them lying naked on the library floor flashed in her head.

"Not at all," said Ben. "I've spent a lot of time traveling in the Far East for work. This is something that I studied while I was there. I enjoy giving and getting massages."

Sinclair knew this was crazy, standing in her aunt's library, letting Ben's hands work their magic, but she couldn't stop him. She was powerless to push him away. She didn't want him to stop. She never wanted him to stop. She let him lead her to the couch, and she sat down obediently, her back to him as he started massaging her lower back.

She couldn't help herself as she let out a moan. "That feels wonderful," she said, forgetting for just a moment the mess her sister was now in. Then a feeling of guilt shattered her feelings of well-being.

"We shouldn't be doing this," said Sinclair. "We need to focus on Everett and Roxie."

Ben continued massaging her back. "First, we're not *doing* anything—at least, not yet. Second, you can't help your sister if you fall apart."

"I'm not falling apart," Sinclair insisted.

"When you walked in here, I could tell that you were barely keeping it together, Sinclair. It's okay to be vulnerable, baby."

She usually hated when men called her "baby," but the word on Ben's lips was like a silken caress. For some inexplicable reason, Sinclair felt hot tears burn in her eyes. His kindness almost made her lose her loosely held self-control. Seeing the anguish in her sister's eyes had affected Sinclair, but she'd known that if she lost it, then Roxie would lose it, too. She needed to stay strong for her sister.

"How is your sister?" Ben asked, still slowly massaging her lower back.

"Not good," Sinclair replied. "How's Everett?"

Ben started rubbing her shoulders. "The same."

"What a mess," said Sinclair.

"It's not good," Ben agreed. "But they'll recover. Life goes on, and people pick up and move on with their lives."

Sinclair turned and faced Ben. "That sounds pretty callous to me."

"Believe me, I'm not being callous," Ben replied. "I know what I'm talking about. You learn to live with what you thought would kill you."

Sinclair understood. She'd had to learn to live with what she thought would kill her—Wayne's betrayal. When her marriage ended, she'd thought that her world would come to a dramatic, screeching halt. Her laughter had died as she watched the unraveling of her world. The pain had been unbearable, and then one day, almost without her realizing it, she'd learned to bear the pain, and she'd learned to laugh again.

"Did someone break your heart?" Sinclair asked, looking into his guarded eyes.

He gave her a wry smile. "You could say that."

"I'm sorry." Sinclair couldn't imagine anyone getting close enough to Ben to break his heart. He struck her as the kind who guarded his heart from all possible penetration.

He looked back at her. "I'm sorry, too."

She leaned forward and kissed him lightly on the cheek. It was a kiss meant to give comfort, not ignite passion, but as she pulled away, Sinclair could see the passion blaze in his eyes. He caught her wrists in his hands and held them tight.

Staring into her eyes, he asked her, "What the hell are you doing to me?"

Sinclair shook her head, confused. She had no idea what he was talking about.

Ben continued. "You make me think about possibilities. I haven't thought about possibilities in a very long time."

He was talking in riddles. Sinclair felt the heat in her stomach flow through the rest of her body. She knew that she was in trouble. Deep trouble.

Licking her lips nervously, Sinclair said, "I think I should go to bed."

Ben didn't let go. "Why are you always running away from me?" he asked.

"I'm not running away," Sinclair said, her voice

breathless. "I just think we need to put a little space between us. . . ."

"Why?" Ben asked, slowly pulling her closer to him.

"Because the last thing we should be thinking about is making love," she blurted out.

"Do you want to make love to me?" he asked.

"Yes," she whispered. "I do."

He gave her a wide smile; then his lips crashed down on hers. It was a kiss unlike the others they'd shared. There was passion in those kisses, but in this kiss, there was possession. She felt as if Ben had put his stamp on her.

She kissed him back, abandoning all common sense. She couldn't think about anything except how good it felt to be in Ben Easington's arms. She didn't know how long she sat on her aunt's couch, kissing Ben, but at some point, she felt Ben pulling away.

"Come with me to my room," he said.

"I'm not sure I should do this," Sinclair said.

"You don't want to feel good when your sister's feeling bad," Ben said.

"Yes." Sinclair nodded.

"Baby, when something good comes your way, you need to reach out and grab it. You don't know how long it's going to stick around. It might go away while you wait."

"How do I know you're something good?"

"You're just going to have to trust me, Sinclair."

"I don't trust easily. I've had bad luck with men."

"I understand that," Ben said, pulling her back into his arms. "But your luck's about to change."

Chapter 16

The sun had risen when Cassius left his room for his morning walk, but just barely. He'd been following this ritual for years. Ever since he'd returned to Jamaica after his divorce, he had gotten up in the morning, no matter how late he'd gone to bed the night before, and walked. He'd often joked that his morning walks were his own personal form of therapy. His joke wasn't too far off from the truth.

He walked down the narrow dirt road that followed the base of the mountain range. He'd thought his sister was just short of crazy when she'd moved here to open her inn. The terrain was beautiful, but it was remote and difficult to get to. But the blue mountains and the lush countryside were seductive. There was also a feeling of tranquility, which was as much an attraction as the beauty of the place.

Cassius could hear the cocks crowing their morning songs as the sun arose behind the mountains. Jamaica was a beautiful place. The harsh economic realities and political challenges that were now an integral part of the country could not take away from the natural beauty of the place. The original settlers on the island, the Arawaks, had named the island Xamayca, which meant "the land of wood and water," and even here in the mountains, Cassius could hear the sounds of a nearby spring. Growing up in Jamaica, he'd taken its beauty for granted, but after returning home, he'd never made that mistake again.

One of his greatest failures, in his opinion, was that he'd never been able to pass down his love of Jamaica to his daughters. To be fair, they hadn't spent much time on the island, but he'd hoped that they realized that a good part of their heritage was in this land. Still, while he knew they enjoyed their time visiting him on the island, they didn't feel the strong connection to this land and its people. He wondered if things would have been different if he'd stayed with Belinda Rose, but he'd had no choice in the matter. Belinda Rose had asked him to exit her life and the lives of his children. Cassius's pride wouldn't allow him to stay where he wasn't wanted. But pride was a lonely bedfellow. Even now, he wished things could have been different. They'd loved each other fiercely, *once upon a time*. But as his late father would say often: "If wishes were horses, then beggars would ride."

He'd made many mistakes in his marriage, including putting his career front and center when that spot should have been taken by his family. As he continued his walk down the dirt road, he wondered if his children were paying the price of his and his wife's inability to keep their family together. Sinclair had chosen a man who was unsuitable for her in every way and had proceeded to marry him. Their divorce was inevitable. As for Roxie, she'd chosen a good man, and then she'd proceeded to hurt him by doing something that was just unimaginable. And, that good man was about to walk out of Roxie's life.

He'd had a brief talk with Everett after Roxie had told him the truth. His son-in-law had been understandably devastated. "Don't make any life decisions when you're this angry," Cassius had advised Everett, but he knew that Everett's pain prevented him from taking any advice.

Cassius couldn't understand Roxie's actions. She was clearly in love with Everett. He knew that his daughter's feelings for her husband were genuine, but she'd thrown away their happiness with one reckless action that would have lifelong ramifications. A baby. He was going to be a grandfather. He'd been looking forward to this moment for some time, but somehow he hadn't imagined that things would turn out this way.

Still, he loved his daughter, and he would love her child. This child was part of his blood. This child was his and Belinda Rose's grandchild, and Cassius was going to make sure that his grandchild knew that he was loved. He didn't know how things would work out between Everett and Roxie, but that didn't matter in the long run. What mattered was, his youngest child was going to have a baby, and Cassius was going to be a part of the baby's life.

He wasn't going to make the same mistakes that he'd made with his own children. He wasn't going to let anyone stop him from developing a relationship with his grandchild. In some respects, he felt as if God had given him a second chance—a chance to be there, fully engaged in the lives of his children and his grandchild—and Cassius was bound and determined not to let this chance pass him by.

He veered off the dirt road and followed a winding walking path at the base of the mountains. After about an hour and a half of brisk walking, Cassius turned around and started walking back toward his sister's inn. Glancing at his watch, he saw that it was almost seven o'clock. He wanted to get back to the inn to be there when Roxie and Sinclair woke up. He had to admit that although the circumstances were dicey, he was glad to have his two girls with him in the land he loved.

Roxie hadn't been able to say much to him yesterday; she'd been too distraught. Today he was going to gently urge Roxie to walk with him, to take in the beauty of the place. He was going to show her that although cheating on someone you loved was not the way that one should, in general, go about doing things, life was about second chances, second acts. She was going to be a mother and she needed to take care of herself, and he was there to help her in this process. He felt his spirits lift, and he quickened his pace.

Rounding the corner, he saw that there was a taxicab parked in front of his sister's inn. This must be one of Beryl's guests, an early arrival, he reasoned, but as he got closer to the inn, he could see that this was no tourist ready to spend some time in one of the most beautiful parts of the island. He could see very clearly that his ex-wife, Belinda Rose, had come to the inn, and from the mutinous expression on her face, she wasn't happy.

His heart literally skipped a beat when he saw her. She was standing by the cab, giving the harried-looking cabdriver directions about her luggage. She looked up as he approached and frowned when she saw him. Cassius had often wondered why, after all this time, his ex-wife still had such a powerful pull on his emotions. After all this time, after all the water that had gone under the bridge and all that, he still loved this woman as much as he'd loved her when he'd first met her years ago.

She was dressed in a linen white dress, which was rumpled from the taxi drive. Her hair had been pulled back in a severe bun, but several strands of hair had escaped the tight bonds and were now blowing about her face, making her look even more beautiful, if that was possible. Her face was devoid of any make-up, but Belinda Rose would always be the most beautiful woman on the planet as far as he was concerned.

He walked over to the cabdriver and barely managed to suppress a smile. Belinda Rose had obviously tried this man's patience. It was what she was good at, bossing people around and speaking her mind.

"I'll take her luggage in," Cassius said.

The cabdriver looked instantly relieved. It was clear that he wanted to get away from Belinda Rose as quickly as possible.

"How much do I owe you?" Cassius asked the driver. "I'll go inside and get my wallet."

"I've already paid the man!" Belinda Rose snapped.

The cabdriver quickly took out the remaining

luggage and placed it on the ground next to the cab. Then, he practically sprinted back into the driver's seat. Cassius smiled as the cabdriver burned rubber in his hasty retreat. Knowing his ex-wife, he couldn't say that he blamed the cab-driver for his actons.

Belinda Rose stood with her hands on her hips. "I don't know what you're grinning about," she said crossly. "Our daughter is in the midst of a scandal, and we're about to be grandparents. Roxie called me with that wonderful news yesterday."

Cassius couldn't help himself. He pulled his ex-wife into his arms and gave her a hug. He held her tight.

"Let me go, you old fool!" Belinda Rose hissed.

Despite her harsh words, Cassius refused to take offense. He knew that his ex-wife was over-whelmed and scared. She loved her daughters, just as he did. He knew that she'd been worried sick about Roxie. Most people didn't know that his tough-talking wife had a soft heart. Once, he'd caught her crying inconsolably when she'd heard about a young mother who'd lost her child. The mother didn't have money to bury her child, and Belinda Rose had arranged for a funeral home to take care of everything, with Belinda Rose footing the entire bill.

Belinda Rose didn't know the woman, but the woman's story had moved her. She'd sworn Cassius to secrecy. "I don't want people to know my busi-ness," she'd told him, but Cassius knew that she didn't want people to know that she had a soft side. Like their daughter Sinclair, Belinda Rose was often on the lookout for people who would take advantage of her kindness. He understood Sinclair's mistrust of people—specifically, men. The two men Sinclair had loved, her father and her husband, had walked out on her. But Cassius had never understood Belinda Rose's natural mistrust of mankind in general, and of him in particular.

He released her reluctantly from his arms.

"This is all your fault!" Belinda Rose snapped, her eyes narrow with disapproval.

She was baiting him, but he refused to take the bait. He was happy that she was here, dammit. She knew her daughter was in trouble, and the mother hen that Belinda Rose was had propelled her to come help her baby.

"How is this *my* fault?" Cassius asked. "Belinda Rose, be reasonable. There's nothing I did to encourage Roxie to cheat on Everett or to leave him."

"You raised her to be weak!"

"I didn't raise her," Cassius said softly.

Belinda Rose kept on talking, as if she hadn't heard Cassius's words. "You were too soft on the girls, both of them! Raising them to think that the world is a good place!"

He wanted to take her in his arms again. He wanted to shut her up with his kisses, but he remained still.

"The world is a good place, Belinda Rose. Sometimes bad things happen, but the world is fundamentally filled with good people."

"That's the kind of reasoning that got my daughter pregnant!"

"I'm not sure I follow you."

"Obviously, the way you raised Roxie helped her to become this weak woman . . . a woman who would give in to her carnal desires . . . when she should have remained strong! I believe, as sure as I am standing here, that this Phillip fellow sensed her weakness and pounced on her . . . literally and figuratively . . . and now we're going to be grandparents, grandparents to a child who will not know who its father is!"

"Roxie made a mistake," Cassius admitted, "but this is her mistake. Not mine. Not yours. I haven't lived with Roxie since she was seven."

"You were there during her formative years!" Belinda Rose said, her eyebrows raised in clear disapproval.

He wasn't going to win this fight.

"What are we going to do?" Belinda Rose wailed.

"We're going to support Roxie, and we're going to support Everett, if he lets us, and we're going to love our grandchild."

Ben woke up to an empty bed and the sound of crowing cocks. He distinctly remembered going to sleep in Sinclair's arms. He'd anticipated waking up in them, and he was disappointed. She was always running away, not that he could blame her. With everything that was going on with her sister, he was sure that she had more important things on her mind than a renewed bout of lovemaking. He was sure that even at this early hour, Sinclair was with her sister. It was one of the things he admired about Sinclair, her loyalty and her love for her family. Even as he'd grumbled about them coming to Jamaica to rescue Roxie, he knew that if he'd faced the same circumstances, he would have done the same thing. It was why he was here with Everett. He hadn't thought that it made sense to run after a woman who had run away, but if his friend was going to make the journey, Ben knew that he'd have to die and be born again before he'd let his best friend face this alone.

When Leneta left for California, taking Ben's little girl with her, Everett had been there for him. Ben valued loyalty; it seemed that lately loyalty was a rare commodity. Everett had gotten him through some tough, dark times. The loneliness that ate at him when Africa moved would have overwhelmed him if Everett hadn't been there to talk with him, and even at times pray with him. Ben wished that he could be that source of support for Everett, but he wasn't sure. Everett was inconsolable. His whole world had come crashing down on him, and Ben was worried that Everett couldn't take the weight of everything that was facing him.

Everett hadn't been able to do much speaking. When Ben had gone to Everett's room, he'd found a broken man. Ben had searched for the right words to say, but there was no way to make this situation nice and neat. The woman Everett loved and had just married was very likely carrying another man's baby. Ben struggled to be charitable to Roxie, but he couldn't understand how she could have gone through the charade of a wedding. He understood that things happened, and sometimes babies came unexpectedly. Africa hadn't been a planned baby, but she was loved from day one. How could Roxie, knowing that she could be carrying another man's baby, not give this information to Everett? And then, to make matters even worse, her disappearing act only confounded an already bad situation.

After leaving Everett, he'd spent a few hours in the darkened library, feeling helpless and angry. There was also another emotion that he'd grappled with: he missed Sinclair. He realized that he'd been lonely for some time. To be honest, he had probably been lonely all his life. He had always been surrounded by people, but still he always felt alone in a crowd. One of the reasons that he traveled so frequently was to get away from his loneliness. The only times that he could remember when loneliness had been kept at bay were the times he spent with his daughter, Africa, and the times he spent with Sinclair.

Sinclair made him laugh. She made him angry. She exasperated him. She challenged him. She drove him crazy. But he couldn't be in the same room with her without wanting to touch her, grab her, kiss her, tickle her, tease her. He craved contact with her. He recognized a kindred lonely spirit. From the time he first saw her, standing out on that patio, he could sense the loneliness that hovered close by. She was also hurt, and justifiably wary of men, but he was going to show her that he was different. He wasn't going to cut and run when the going got tough. Sinclair felt like something he was searching for—she felt like home—and he wasn't going to let that go, at least not easily.

He knew she'd put up a fight. She was attracted to him, but she'd fought her attraction every step of the way. Well, he thought as he stretched in the comfortable antique sleigh bed, he was a formidable foe. She wasn't going to win this fight. He'd show her that they belonged together. He was going to show her that he was the man she should be waking up next to for the next fifty years, God willing.

But first he needed to check on Everett. It was still early—the clock on the wall showed that it was just past seven thirty—but Ben was certain that Everett hadn't had much sleep last night. Neither had he—but for very different reasons. After a night of what he could best describe as spectacular lovemaking, he'd fallen asleep at about four in the morning. His body was tired, but his mind was energized.

He was going to go to Everett and force him to get out of bed. Maybe they'd take a walk or a morning swim in the pool in the back of the inn. He'd make Everett eat. Ben followed his grandmother's saying that life always looked better when one had a full stomach. He was going to show Everett that this was not the end of him. It was a tough situation, but it was a situation that Ben was not going to allow Everett to face alone.

Then, when he got the chance, he was going to kiss Sinclair until she was breathless. He was going to show her that life does indeed go on, and he intended to convince her to be a part of his life. But knowing Sinclair, he knew that this wasn't going to be easy. He only hoped that she would let down those carefully constructed walls she'd placed all around her, and let him in.

Chapter 17

Just when Sinclair thought life couldn't get any more complicated, her mother arrived on the scene. Sinclair had spoken to her mother yesterday, but her mother hadn't told her about any plans to come to Jamaica. While Sinclair understood her mother's need to be near Roxie, especially since Roxie was hurting, she knew her mother's presence would complicate an already complicated situation. First, her mother wasn't overly fond of Jamaica, Aunt Beryl, or her father—though not necessarily in that order. Second, her mother's tendency to be dramatic and overwrought was definitely the last thing Roxie needed. Third, her mother was just plain old crazy at times, and there was just no stopping her when the craziness hit, and the craziness had clearly already arrived.

"We've got to get Roxie away from here," her mother was whispering to her. "Once we get her away from these people, we can talk some sense into her!"

Sinclair and her mother were sitting in Sinclair's

room, on her bed. After her mother had arrived, she'd demanded to know where Sinclair was, and she'd marched up to her room. Thank God, Sinclair had left Ben's room. Two daughters of ill repute might just push her mother over the edge.

"Mom"—Sinclair tried to use her let's-be-reasonable voice—"these people that you're referring to are her family."

"*They* are the reason for her loose behavior!" her mother declared. "Beryl was a woman of easy virtue for years! That stint in the nunnery clearly didn't do much for her, and you know Roxie has probably been confiding in her!"

Sinclair shook her head. A woman of easy virtue? Who talked that way? "Aunt Beryl is a wonderful, free-spirited woman," said Sinclair, defending her aunt.

Her mother was undeterred. "It's that free spirit that probably encouraged my daughter to lie down with that horrible man and to cheat on Everett!"

Sinclair let out a sigh. Crazy had definitely set up residence with her mother. Hysteria couldn't be too far behind.

"And your father!" Her mother continued her tirade. "He spoiled both of you!"

"How did I get in this?" Sinclair asked. "What did I do?"

"He should have guided both of you girls with a firmer hand. It would have made you both stronger."

"Mom, we're women. Our mistakes are our own."

Her mother let out a derisive snort. "I am not going to argue with you, Sinclair Evonne."

This was serious. Her mother only used her middle name in times of extreme crisis.

"Mom, exactly what do you think we should be doing?"

"We need to take Roxie back to New York. She can think clearly in New York. She can decide what she's going to do about the baby."

Sinclair felt her blood run cold. Surely, her mother wasn't suggesting that Roxie not have her baby. "Mom, Roxie's going to keep her baby."

"I know that!" her mother snapped. "But she's going to have to figure out what she's going to do about her job. Of course, she's going to have to move in with me. She can't raise that baby by herself! Everett's not going to want to have anything to do with her or the baby!"

"Roxie is perfectly capable of making these decisions herself," said Sinclair. "Our job is to support her."

"Thanks, Sis."

Neither Sinclair nor her mother had noticed that Roxie had entered the room.

"Hi, Mom," said Roxie. She sounded tired, but she sounded stronger than she had the day before. "Dad told me you were here."

"How are you, baby?" Her mother's voice softened as she took in the sight of Roxie in an oversized men's T-shirt and jeans.

Roxie sat in the chair adjacent to the bed on which Sinclair and her mother were sitting.

"I've been better," said Roxie. "But I'm hanging in there."

"Roxie, I think that you and Sinclair should come back to New York with me," said her mother.

"You came all this way to tell me this?" Roxie asked.

"I came to take you back," replied her mother.

"Mom, I think Sinclair should go back with you, but I'm staying here. I want to have my baby in Jamaica," said Roxie.

"What!" Her mother's voice, already high-pitched, rose two octaves. The expression on her face showed that she couldn't be more surprised or disapproving if Roxie had suggested giving birth on the moon. "That is absolutely out of the question."

Sinclair watched as her sister underwent a transformation. The old Roxie would have cowered and given in. The old Roxie would have pouted. The old Roxie would have cried. But this Roxie sat with perfect posture and kept her voice even and cool when she replied to her irate mother.

"I will be having my baby here in Jamaica," said Roxie. "Dad is going to refer me to an obstetrician, and this is where my child is going to be born."

"But why?" her mother wailed.

Roxie continued. "Because I want my child to be born in the beautiful land of his ancestors. There's nothing for me in New York right now. Everett has made it clear that he doesn't want anything to do with me, not that I blame him. I've explained everything to my job, and I've taken a leave of absence for the rest of the year."

"What about insurance for you and the baby?" her mother asked, apparently grasping at any reason to spirit her daughter off of the island.

"Dad is going to take care of all of the expenses," Roxie replied. "Of course, I'll pay him back every penny."

Sinclair's mother turned and faced her. "I told you that her father was encouraging her in this madness!"

"Mom, Dad has been wonderful and supportive, just as I'd hoped you'd be," Roxie said, her voice clear and unwavering.

"You can't just take a leave of absence from your job. They need you," cried her mother. She was clearly getting desperate. She'd never approved of Roxie's career as an interior decorator with one of New York's top design houses.

"They're fine with this," said Roxie. "But even if they weren't fine, that's not going to change my decision. I've got to do what is in the best interest of my child, and I believe that is me staying here in Jamaica with Dad and Aunt Beryl."

"I'll stay with you," Sinclair said. She wasn't going to let her sister face being pregnant and giving birth somewhere far away.

Roxie gave her sister a small smile. "I appreciate the offer, Sis, but you have a life you need to get back to. You don't need to baby-sit me. I'll be fine."

And as Sinclair looked into her sister's serene green eyes, she knew that Roxie was right. No matter how tough the next few months got, Roxie was going to be fine.

"You'll be sorry," her mother declared ominously.

Roxie's smile grew wider. "No, I won't," she replied. "I've never been more sure of anything in my entire life."

"That's what you said about marrying Everett,"

her mother intoned. "And look at where both of you are today!"

"Mom!" Sinclair cried and shook her head. Sometimes her mother's mouth didn't catch up with her head. "What an awful thing to say!"

"The truth is the light!" her mother declared, suddenly calling on her Baptist roots with that particular saying.

"Mom, I understand that. based on my past actions, you probably don't have a lot of faith in me," said Roxie. "I didn't have any faith in myself until recently. But, Mom, trust me, this is the right decision for me, and more importantly, it's the right decision for my baby. I have a strong faith. God is going to see me and my baby through."

"Where was this faith when you were cheating on your husband-to-be?" her mother asked, with one censuring eyebrow raised.

Sinclair couldn't help it. Laughter rose in her throat and threatened to escape. Her mother had a point—a deliciously wicked and incredibly funny point. Folks tended to cling to Jesus when they got caught in wrongdoing. Sinclair started coughing to cover her laughter up, but as she looked over at Roxie, she could see that Roxie was laughing, too.

"I don't see what both of you are laughing about!" cried their mother.

"No," said Roxie, after her laughter subsided, "you wouldn't, but we love you, anyway."

Sinclair watched as her mother narrowed her eyes. "Your bed doesn't look as if anyone slept in it. Where were you last night, Sinclair?"

Damn. Her mother was better than the FBI and the CIA rolled up into one.

Sinclair watched as her sister flashed a wide smile. "She was with me, Mom. Safe and sound."

Her mother's narrowed eyes clearly showed that she didn't believe a word Roxie said.

Ben found the person he was looking for in the garden. Sinclair was sitting on one of the white wrought-iron benches in the garden, holding a book in her hand. She'd been engrossed in whatever it was she was reading, and it wasn't until he was almost beside her that she looked up. The spontaneous smile she gave him made his insides grow warm. She was wearing jeans, with a loose-fitting white top, which was blowing in the light breeze. Her gold hoop earrings dangled enticingly on her ears. While he felt sweaty and slightly uncomfortable, Sinclair looked cool and refreshed—despite the heat. Although it was only midmorning, the temperature was hotter than Ben was used to, and he was grateful for the breeze.

"What are you reading?" Ben asked, sitting next to her.

She grinned at him. "I'm reading *The Difficult Pet*. I'm trying to give my mind a mental vacation."

He laughed out loud. "What about a romance or a mystery? Don't you ever get away from your work?"

"I love romances, and I love mysteries," Sinclair replied, moving closer to him. "But I also love books about animals. This book is really great. You should read it. It's a sequel to *The Misunderstood Pet*."

He reached over and pulled her to his side. Planting a light kiss on her forehead, Ben said,

"Since I don't intend on ever having a pet in this lifetime, I think I'll pass on both of those books, as riveting as they sound."

"Your loss," said Sinclair. "You don't know what you're missing."

"Speaking of which," Ben said as he inhaled her scent of light spice and vanilla, "I missed you this morning. You've got to stop running from my bed."

Sinclair giggled. "One scandal in my family is plenty, thank you very much. If they found us sleeping together, my father would worry, and my mother would be appalled. They have enough on their plate without me adding any more drama."

"We're adults, Sinclair," Ben reasoned. "Not teenagers sneaking around."

"Trust me on this," Sinclair replied. "They wouldn't see it that way. And now that my mother's arrived, it's probably best that we keep a little distance. I don't want my mom in my business."

"So," Ben said softly, still teasing, "we've got business now?"

Sinclair cleared her throat, clearly embarrassed. "In a manner of speaking."

He looked down and saw Sinclair's sexy brown feet. Everything about her was sexy—the way she challenged him, her reading esoteric books on pet behavior, her gold hoop earrings, her full rosebud lips. Everything. But there were a lot of sexy women. For Ben, Sinclair's allure was more powerful than that. She made him want to do right. She made him want to please her. She made him want to protect her, although if he were honest, he'd admit that he was more in need of protection than she was. She hadn't given him her heart yet, but his heart was long gone, and it belonged to Sinclair. He was not going to let this woman slip away.

"Sinclair, will you be my girl?"

She looked up at him and smiled. "Aren't I a little old to be your girl?" she teased.

Ben leaned over and kissed her lips lightly; then he pulled away. "I want you to be in my life, Sinclair. You choose the capacity. If you want me to be a friend, I'll be a friend. If you want me to be more, and I'm hoping you do, then I'll be more."

"You're serious about this?" she asked.

Ben nodded his head. "Very serious," he replied. He didn't want to scare her, and he could tell by Sinclair's eyes that she was afraid. It made him angry to think about the man who had caused the fear and mistrust in her eyes. Her ex-husband had made things difficult for the next man in Sinclair's life, and Ben intended to be the next man in her life.

Sinclair stared at him. "I don't know," she said. "The timing's kind of bad, Ben. My sister needs me."

"I understand that," Ben replied. "And I'll support that. But I still want you in my life."

"Let me think about this," she replied. This was not the response that he wanted, but she hadn't turned him down. He still had hope.

"How is your sister?" Ben asked, changing the subject. Sinclair was obviously uncomfortable with talk about the possibility of a relationship.

"She's better," Sinclair replied. Ben could see her visibly relaxing now that the conversation had changed. "How's Everett?"

"Not better," said Ben. "He wants to leave the

island as soon as possible. We're booked on a flight leaving Montego Bay tomorrow."

"You're leaving, too?" Sinclair asked.

Ben wasn't sure if he'd imagined it, but Sinclair looked disappointed.

"I didn't think that you'd be leaving this soon," Sinclair nodded.

"Our taxi should be here any minute. We're driving back to St. Christopher. Your father offered to let us stay at his place. His driver will take us to the airport tomorrow."

He watched as Sinclair tried to be stoic, but he could see that she was hurt. There was also something else in her eyes: resignation. Yet another man was leaving her.

"Baby, I'm only going to New York. I'm not walking out of your life," he said softly.

"It's okay," Sinclair replied, but Ben could tell it wasn't okay.

He leaned over again and gave her a deep kiss. He wanted to convey in that kiss what he obviously couldn't convey in words—that he wasn't going anywhere. He needed to be in New York with his friend, just as she needed to be in Jamaica with her sister. But he was here for the long run. He was here for better and for worse.

He felt her responding to his kiss. The passion between them was undeniable. He deepened the kiss, thrusting his tongue deftly into her waiting mouth. He tasted her, and for one crazy moment, he thought about making love to her in the garden. When he finally pulled away, his heart was hammering in his chest.

When he finally trusted that both he and his

voice were under control, Ben said, "Would a man getting ready to walk out of your life kiss you that way?"

He was rewarded with a sly grin. "Actually, you'd be surprised. Wayne made love to me the night before he announced he was leaving me."

"I'm going to tell you this once, and I'll hopefully never have to tell you this again. My name is Ben. Benjamin David Easington. I'm not Wayne. We are two very different men."

"I'm sorry," Sinclair said. "There's a Jamaican saying that my dad says all the time: 'If a snake bites you, rope scares you.' I know that you're not Wayne. I'm sorry."

"Don't be sorry, baby. Just find me when you get back to New York."

They heard the sound of an approaching car.

Ben stood up. "That's probably the taxi."

Sinclair stood up also. "I'll come with you."

Ben pulled her into his arms and held her tight. He didn't want to leave her. He was already missing Sinclair. But he needed to be with Everett. He and Sinclair had a lifetime to be together. He knew he'd found the woman he wanted to marry. He just hoped he could convince her to give marriage another try. Well, first things first. He had to convince her that he was a good man; a man who wasn't going to walk out on her; a man who would never, in this lifetime or the next, cheat on her; and a man who was going to be waiting for her in New York.

Chapter 18

Sinclair watched the taxi drive away. She had an inexplicable urge to burst into tears. No matter what she'd shared with Ben, she still hardly knew the man. True, they'd had some passionate nights, and the attraction between them was nothing like she'd ever experienced, but this feeling of desolation that came crashing down on her, as the taxi carrying Ben and Everett made its way down the hill, troubled her. It wasn't like her to get so attached, especially given her history with men. They'd only known each other a few days, and here she was, acting like a woman in love who'd just lost her man.

Shaking her head, she turned around, intending to walk back to the inn. She saw her sister standing there. Roxie looked as stricken as Sinclair felt. While Everett and Ben had gotten ready to leave, Roxie had stayed out of sight. She'd told Sinclair that she didn't want to make a tough situation tougher. She knew that her presence would cause Everett pain. Now that he was gone, Roxie had emerged from her room. The confidence with which she'd faced her mother was now gone. She looked like a little girl.

"What have I done?" Roxie asked.

Sinclair walked beside her sister and linked her arm through Roxie's arm. "Let's go and feed my little niece or my nephew some good Jamaican food."

"Do you think Everett will ever forgive me?" Roxie asked.

"I don't know," Sinclair answered honestly. "But I know that he's a good man. He doesn't have it in his heart to hold on to bad feelings about you. Give him time."

Roxie let out a small sigh. "I know this sounds foolish, but I never meant to hurt him. It was just something crazy that happened."

"Nothing just happens." Sinclair tried to be as gentle as possible, but she wanted Roxie to stop fooling herself. People didn't just happen to cheat. There might be a myriad of reasons for infidelity, but it never "just happened," at least in her experience. "There's a reason why you did this, and maybe now is as good a time as any to find out."

"You're right. I guess I've got the next five months to find out."

"And I'll be right here with you," said Sinclair. She was going to have to call the station to see what could be worked out. The animal clinic and daycare for dogs were already in good hands. She had to think of what she was going to do with her own dog. She couldn't go five months without Princess.

Roxie stopped walking. "No, you won't," she said.

"I told you this morning, I didn't want you to baby-sit me, Sis."

"Is that what you think I'm doing?"

"Something like that," said Roxie. "You need to get back to your life. And something tells me there's a person in New York that you might want to get back to."

"If you're referring to Ben, that's nothing," Sinclair replied, quickly feeling embarrassed. She didn't want to think that she was an uncaring person who was carrying on a wild flirtation while her sister's life fell apart.

"It didn't look like nothing to me," Roxie replied. "From what I saw going on in the garden . . . well, let's just say, I was tempted to tell you both to get a room!"

"Oh God," Sinclair groaned. "Was it that bad?"

"Are you kidding me?" Roxie asked, with an impish smile. "I think it's wonderful! It's high time you got laid."

Her mother was right. Her baby sister really was scandalous. "It's good to see you smiling," Sinclair said in an attempt to change the subject.

"Ben is a good man, Sinclair," Roxie continued. "Don't make the same mistake I did."

"What mistake is that?"

"Taking a good man for granted."

"It's not what you think," Sinclair said hastily. Her sister's talk about Ben was making her distinctly nervous. She liked him. She liked him a lot. But she didn't want to like him. She wasn't ready for anything. Her heart was still healing. She didn't want Wayne back, but the remnants from the storm he blew through her life were still hanging around.

"Don't let Wayne stop you from finding happiness. He didn't let you stop him from doing any damn thing he pleased."

Her sister had a very good point there. "Could we talk about something different?"

"Okay." Roxie let that uncomfortable subject drop. "But I want you to go back to New York, Sinclair."

"Why're you trying to get rid of me?" Sinclair asked.

"Because you've been coming to my rescue since I was a little girl, Sinclair. It's time for me to come to my own rescue. I'll be fine. I'll be with Dad and Aunt Beryl. You can come visit me, but you need to get on with your own life. You're so busy trying to rescue everyone else. You need to rescue yourself, Sinclair. You need to stop putting everything on hold while life passes you by. It's time, Sis."

"But I don't want to leave you," said Sinclair. Roxie was right on many different levels. Sinclair had been taking care of her sister for years. It was what she believed she needed to do, especially after that dark time when their father moved away to Jamaica. She didn't want to leave her sister in Jamaica. But Roxie was right. She was going to be a mother, and if this was what she felt she needed to do, then Sinclair had to respect her sister's wishes. Roxie was also right about Sinclair keeping her life on hold while she waited to get over whatever it was she thought she'd lost when Wayne walked out of her life. Looking back, she saw that she hadn't lost anything.

Wayne hadn't been good for her, nor had he been good to her, but her stubborn loyalty gene had prevented her from doing what he had ultimately done—walk out on the marriage. He'd done her a big favor, but that hadn't stopped her from being hurt about it. But she'd used the hurt as a protective shield, which was keeping her from developing a relationship with another man. Her life had been safe and predictable, two things she'd craved. Still, there was something missing. She wasn't the kind of woman that believed that having a man was a prerequisite to happiness. She knew better. Years with Wayne had taught her this painful lesson. Still, it was one thing to be without a relationship by choice. She was without a relationship because of fear. There was a difference. She had to stop being afraid.

Sinclair thought about Ben. She was afraid of him. She was afraid of her feelings for him. The last time she'd given her heart to someone, she'd ended up getting burned. This time she would, hopefully, be older and wiser. She'd seen problems in Wayne before they'd gotten married, but she'd convinced herself that his love for her would straighten all the problems out. She didn't see any of those signs with Ben, but she didn't know him.

"Give Ben a chance," said Roxie. "Give yourself a chance. It's not like you have to marry the guy."

Sinclair looked at her sister. "I still don't want to leave you."

"I know," Roxie replied. "But I'm going to be fine. One more thing, Sis."

"What is it?" Sinclair asked.

"Please take Mom with you."

* * *

Everett watched the Jamaican countryside whiz by in a green blur. Since Roxie had told him about the baby, he'd felt as if he were in a deep fog. He was angry, and he was hurt, but it was much more than that. He was devastated. Almost from the moment he'd met Roxie, he'd known that he wanted to make her his wife. She was seemingly everything he'd ever wanted in a woman—kind, beautiful, smart, funny—and she loved him back. He couldn't believe his incredible luck in finding her, and to know that she loved him. Now he knew that it was all an act. The relationship. The wedding vows. Their future plans together. It was all a lie.

He felt the air leave his lungs. He couldn't breathe. He rolled the window down and tried to get more air. It had been years since he'd had a panic attack. He'd thought he'd conquered these attacks. He saw he was wrong.

He felt Ben's steadying hand on his shoulder. "Take it easy, Ev. Just try to breathe." Ben was one of the few people outside his family who knew about Everett's panic attacks. He'd never told Roxie about them. He'd been afraid that she'd think he was weak. Now he realized that she probably wouldn't have cared one way or the other. But how could she have kept up this act for so long? Was there ever a time that she genuinely loved him? he wondered.

Everett shook his head, trying to get the thoughts of Roxie out of his head. He felt the panic rising. "Can't," he managed to get out. "Can't breathe."

"Pull the cab over," Everett heard Ben order the driver.

"What you say, mon?" the driver asked.

"My friend isn't feeling well," said Ben. His voice was clipped. "We need to stop."

The driver pulled over to the side of the road.

Everett closed his eyes and tried to concentrate on breathing, but he felt as if the air was being sucked from his throat. He closed his eyes and tried to calm down, but he could feel his heart hammering in his chest. The heat that suffused him was almost unbearable. Was he going to die?

He heard a car door open, and then he opened his eyes to see Ben's concerned face at the passenger door. Ben stretched out his hand. "Come outside," he said.

Ben helped him get to his feet. Everett was suddenly aware of the sound of waves. The road was near the sea. In the distance, Everett could make out the blue water. Ben walked with him and talked with him. All the while, Everett listened to the rhythmic sounds of the sea. He listened to Ben's voice as he talked. The words made no sense to Everett, but the sound of Ben's voice, his steady hand on Everett's shoulder, and the sounds of the waves managed to calm Everett's panic. His breathing returned to normal. He still felt sick, but at least he could breathe.

Everett tried to make a joke about his panic attack. "I thought I was going to die," he said.

"Not on my watch," Ben replied.

"How the hell am I going to get over this?" Everett asked.

Ben shook his head slowly. "I don't know, man. I wish I did."

"The worst thing about all of this is that I still love her," Everett admitted. It was true. His love for her should have come to a crashing halt when she told him about her betrayal. But it hadn't. It continued, wounded and limping, but it continued. He could never trust her again. He could never be with her again. But he knew that he would always love Roxie, and the thought filled him with an unspeakable despair.

"Love is like that, my man," said Ben. "Sometimes it flourishes in the most unlikely of circumstances."

Chapter 19

The next day Ben found himself in an airplane, staring out the window at the New York City skyline. He'd spent most of yesterday talking with Everett. After Everett's panic attack had passed, their conversation seemed to have lifted him out of his stupor. He was still sad, but he was more communicative. They'd spent a relatively quiet time at Cassius Dearheart's house, watching soccer and cricket on the television. The cook had fixed them their meals, and the surroundings were comfortable, but Ben had missed Sinclair. He missed her now, as the airplane began its final descent into JFK Airport.

New York was covered with a gray haze that late afternoon, and the water surrounding the city was gray. He remembered the vivid blue-green water that he'd seen, with the sunlight dancing on the waves, when the airplane had lifted off earlier that morning. New York City was one of Ben's favorite places in the world, but the familiar sight of New York's dramatic skyline failed to raise his spirits. Bcside him, Everett sat quietly, seemingly lost in his thoughts. It was going to be tough going for Everett, but Ben had made himself a promise that he'd be right there with his friend, helping him through this.

The airplane landed with three quick bumps and sped down the runway. He was home. Once the airplane finally reached its gate, Ben gathered his belongings and quickly left the aircraft, with Everett following closely behind him. They cleared customs quickly, and after getting their bags, Ben hailed a cab, which first took Everett to his apartment, located at the southern tip of Manhattan, near Wall Street. Ben had asked his friend if he wanted company, but Everett had declined. It was clear that he wanted to be alone.

As the cab made its way north to Ben's Upper West Side apartment, Ben noticed that his cell phone was buzzing. Because it hadn't worked in Jamaica, he'd put it away and almost forgotten it existed. Taking the cell phone out of the pocket of his jacket, Ben saw the message light blinking. He turned on the phone and saw he had nineteen messages. He dialed his voice mail and listened to the messages—all nineteen of them. Eighteen of the messages were from his ex, Leneta, and one message was from his dry cleaner. His shirts were apparently ready to be picked up.

Leneta had left him messages about their daughter, Africa. Africa hadn't returned from school yesterday, and Leneta suspected that she was hanging out with her boyfriend. According to the third message Leneta left him, Africa had done this a couple of times before. By the eighteenth message, Leneta sounded frantic. Africa was fifteen years old, and Leneta had found birth-control pills in Africa's top drawer. The pills were missing, just as Africa was.

Ben dialed Leneta's number. She answered on the first ring.

"Where the hell have you been?" Leneta demanded.

"Hi. How are you?" Ben replied. "Where's my daughter?"

"I have no idea," said Leneta. "I was finally able to reach Kwame's parents."

"Who's Kwame?" Ben asked. "What does this have to do with Africa?"

"Kwame's her boyfriend," said Leneta. "Didn't you listen to my messages?"

After the first seven messages, Ben had fast-forwarded through the rest of the messages, only listening to highlights, but he thought it best not to let Leneta know. She was already aggravated enough.

Leneta went on. "His parents said that Africa was with him last night, but she flew to see her grandmother."

"Which grandmother?" Ben asked, trying to be patient. Leneta had a way of going around and around until she finally got to the point. "She has two."

"I know how many grandmothers my child has!" Leneta snapped. "She's supposed to be going to my mother's place in Harlem. That's not far from you."

Ben sighed. "At least we know she's safe."

"You need to go over there to make sure she's okay. Then put her on a plane back to California."

"Have you spoken to your mom yet?"

"Yeah, Mom says she hasn't arrived. She's beside herself with worry."

Ben sighed again. "Tell your mom not to worry. Our daughter is as resourceful as she is cunning. How'd she get the money to buy the ticket?"

"I don't know," Leneta replied. "You and Mom are always sending her money. . . ."

"So how are you otherwise?" Ben asked, trying to cut off yet another lecture about his bad parenting skills.

Now it was Leneta's turn to sigh. "These teenage years are hell!" she said. "I don't know what happened to my sweet, agreeable daughter. She's sneaking out to meet boys. Her grades are slipping. She's on birth control, and I haven't seen her in two days."

"She's not a bad kid," said Ben, and that was, in fact, true. On the whole, Africa had a good head on her shoulders. Until recently, her grades had been stellar, she was respectful of her parents, and she had a wicked sense of humor. "She's just going through a phase."

"I'll be glad when this phase is over," Leneta declared. "I just hope I'll live long enough to see her come back to her senses."

After a few more minutes, Ben got off the phone, telling Leneta to have her mother call him when their wayward daughter showed up. He knew that he should be more worried, but he was certain that if any fifteen-year-old could navigate flying across the country without incident, it was his resourceful offspring. Still, he was going to have to have a serious discussion with Africa. She couldn't go around jumping on planes and running away from home when the spirit moved her. Also, this boyfriend situation was something she needed to let go of. She was too young. He was glad that she was responsible enough to use birth control, but the fact remained that at fifteen, she should not be engaging in sex.

The cab pulled up in front of his apartment building, and after paying the driver his fare and a generous tip, Ben grabbed his suitcases and headed for the front door of his building. Hector, his doorman, opened the door.

"Welcome back, Ben," he said. Although Hector called the rest of the residents of the apartment building by their last name, Ben had insisted that Hector call him by his first name. Mr. Easington was his father.

"How's life?" Ben asked as he walked into the building.

"It's pretty good, even though my wife keeps hassling me about losing this weight. She's worried about my cholesterol. I keep telling her that I'm going to live forever."

Ben chuckled. "She's a good woman, Hector. She's just looking out for you."

"I've been out for the past three days," said Hector. "I just got back about half an hour ago. I tell you, I was glad to get to work! I needed a break from all that talk about eating right and exercise. She's even trying to get me to give up my beer. Now that's where I draw the line."

Ben laughed. "Your wife is going to make sure that you stick around. Can't say that I blame her."

The elevator door opened, and Ben said good-bye to Hector. He was suddenly very tired. He wanted to dump his suitcases on the living-room floor in his apartment and head straight to his bed. He thought about calling Leneta's mother in Harlem, but he knew she'd call him as soon as Africa showed up. Then, as the elevator door opened on his floor, he thought about calling Sinclair. When he left the island this morning, the phone lines in the area where Beryl's inn was located were down again.

He walked to his door, feeling the familiar sense of loneliness grip him. Although he welcomed a quiet apartment, there was a part of him that missed the company that Sinclair provided. He missed hearing her voice, and it was only one day. He hoped she'd come back to the city soon, but if she didn't, he was going to have to make another trip to Jamaica.

He searched for the keys in his pocket until he found them. Then, Ben opened the door and got the shock of his life. His daughter, Africa. was standing in the middle of the living room, and in her arms was a small, furry creature—a dog.

While he searched for the right words to say—curses came to mind—his daughter flashed him a beautiful smile, the identical smile her mother would use on him when she wanted to get her way in any particular argument, and said, "Hi, Daddy."

Chapter 20

Sinclair stood on the veranda and watched the sun slide down behind the mountains. Once again, the sound of crickets heralded the approaching evening. The day had passed peacefully enough. Her mother had kept mostly to herself in her room. She'd declared that she was still jet-lagged and needed her sleep. No one complained, and Sinclair was glad for the relative quiet with her mother tucked away in her room.

Roxie had tried to mope around, but neither Sinclair nor Aunt Beryl would allow her to wallow in any more self-pity. They made sure she ate, and they'd all three taken a walk in the afternoon.

"You can't sit around feeling sorry for yourself," Aunt Beryl had declared, and Sinclair had wondered whether her aunt was talking to Roxie or to her.

Aunt Beryl had been wonderful. Pointing out different plants during the walk, and keeping the conversation light, her aunt had managed to ease some of the tension out of Roxie's face. By the time they'd returned home, Roxie was in better spirits, and she'd gone up to her room to freshen up for dinner.

Roxie's renewed appetite was a good sign. For the first two days, she'd hardly eaten anything, but her aunt had cajoled her with freshly squeezed fruit juice and Jamaican comfort food—curried chicken and rice and peas. Even now, as Sinclair stood on the veranda, she could smell something delicious cooking. A honeymooning couple waved at her as they began their walk down the path by the mountains. Sinclair wished that she could spend more time at her aunt's inn, but Roxie was right. She needed to get back home.

She'd decided to come back to Jamaica at some point in the next few months, but it was clear that Roxie would be well taken care of, with her aunt and her father in constant attendance. She'd made arrangements to fly back to New York in a few days. Wondering how Ben was doing, Sinclair sat down on the veranda railing. She hadn't heard from him since he left, but she wasn't surprised. The phone lines were down, and there was no cell-phone service in this remote part of the island. She'd had to travel to the nearest town, Port Antonio, to use the phone to make arrangements for her and her mother to return home.

"A penny for your thoughts," her father said as he walked out on the veranda.

"Hi, Daddy," Sinclair greeted her father. Despite the family drama, it was nice having him around. They didn't spend as much time together as they should, and this time at her aunt's inn had been the most time they'd spent in each other's company in a long while.

"What is my oldest child thinking about?"

"New York," Sinclair replied.

"Oh really." Her father raised an eyebrow. "I thought perhaps you'd be thinking about that Ben fellow, Everett's friend."

Did *everybody* know her business?

"I don't know what would make you feel that I'm thinking about Ben Easington," Sinclair replied, looking away to evade her father's direct stare.

"Well," Cassius replied. "I was born at night, but I wasn't born last night. I've been around long enough to recognize love when I see it."

"Love!" Sinclair exclaimed. "We hardly know each other."

"True enough," said Cassius. "But apparently, that hasn't stopped the both of you from falling in love."

"Dad, you're a hopeless romantic."

"No," Cassius said. "I'm a hopeful one. He seems like a nice guy, Sinclair."

"He's okay," Sinclair said.

"Well, I just want you to know that I approve this time."

"This time?"

Sinclair watched as Cassius leaned back in his chair. "I never approved of your ex-husband. I never kept that a secret from you."

Her father had spoken to her about his reservations concerning Wayne. But Sinclair had rushed headlong into a disastrous marriage. To his credit, her father never said, "I told you so," when Sinclair finally filed for divorce.

"He wants to start seeing me," Sinclair said.

"Looks like that train has already left the station," Cassius commented. "I think you guys are already seeing each other."

"Dad, how do you know when someone is right for you?"

"You'll just know," said Cassius. "Your heart will tell you."

"Aw, Dad, don't get all New Age with me. What exactly does that mean?"

Her father stood up and prepared to leave the veranda.

"You'll know when you know," he said mysteriously, and then he left the veranda.

Sinclair sighed. Why did she expect anyone in her family to give her direct answers? Still, her father usually gave good advice, but today he had definitely missed the mark.

Chapter 21

"What are you doing in my apartment, and why is there a dog in your arms?" Ben asked his daughter as he struggled to keep his voice calm. Not only was this the third dog that had crossed his path in about as many days, but the way that his daughter and the dog were both looking at him, it was clear that they both intended to spend some quality time in his apartment.

Africa put the dog down, but she didn't venture any closer to Ben.

"The doorman let me in. He remembered me."

It had been seven months since he'd last seen his daughter. In those months, Ben could tell that there had been a lot of changes. It was difficult to adjust to the miniskirt, the Birkenstock shoes, the dark brown lipstick, and the stylish, short cut. Where were the jeans and cartoon character T-shirts? This pretty, gum-chewing adolescent looked like his little girl, but he suspected that his little girl had left the scene some time ago, and in her place had appeared a teen on the verge of young womanhood.

Ben put his suitcases down. "Since when did you start wearing lipstick?" he asked. "And since when did you start running away from home? Your mother's worried sick about you."

Africa let out a derisive snort. "Mom doesn't give a damn about me," she said.

"Watch your language," Ben replied. "Your mom's left me nineteen phone messages. That doesn't sound like a worried mom to you?"

"Mom's a control freak. She just wants to control me."

"Someone's got to do it," Ben replied. "Obviously, you're not doing such a hot job right now. Bad grades. Hopping on airplanes and flying cross-country without telling your mom. What if something terrible had happened to you? Do you know how many pedophiles are out there?"

"I knew you'd take her side."

Ben counted to ten slowly. He'd heard about the teenage years being nothing short of torture, but he'd been convinced that his sweet little girl would be immune from the devil, who apparently came calling between the ages of thirteen and nineteen.

Africa walked over to the couch. The dog followed obediently. He watched in amazement as Africa bent down to lift the animal up to sit on the couch with her.

"Don't you dare put that beast on my couch," Ben roared, his patience now worn very thin. He tried to calm down. He hated yelling. "And I'm not taking anyone's side. What you did was wrong, and I'm not going to sugarcoat it. This has nothing to do with taking your mom's side, although she's right, and you, Africa Easington, are dead wrong."

Africa rolled her eyes as she sat down on the couch. The dog wagged its tail hopefully, but Africa wisely refrained from putting him on her father's couch. Ben walked over and sat next to her.

"What's going on with you?" he asked.

"I needed a break from Mom, and I took it."

Ben counted to ten again, afraid that he was going to explode. After traveling all day, and dealing with the aftereffects of the actions of a runaway bride, not to mention the huge ache that came from missing Sinclair, Ben knew that his nerves were worn very thin. He also recognized that something was troubling his daughter, and he didn't want to push her away. He wanted her to confide in him, to let him know what was wrong, and if he came down too hard on her, driving her away might just be the end result. Still, in his day, if he'd done anything quite so crazy, his parents would have reached for the nearest belt.

"Does this have anything to do with the boy you've been dating?" Ben asked, his voice gruff. He'd been a teenager once, and he hated the thought of any boy doing things to his daughter that he'd done to girls those many years ago.

"Yes, and no. She won't let me see him. She says things are too serious."

"Anything that causes you to take birth control at the age of fifteen is too serious for you, Africa."

Africa ducked her head in apparent embarrassment. Although it had been a while since Ben crossed the divide between the teenage years and adulthood, some things remained the same. No teenagers liked to discuss their sex lives with their parents. Hell, no adult really wanted to do that, either. At least he didn't.

"Mom shouldn't have told you that," she said. "She betrayed my confidence."

"She's worried about you."

"Well, she doesn't have to worry anymore. Kwame and I broke up. That's why I came here. I didn't want to face him, and I didn't want to face Mom."

"You ran away because some boy broke your heart?" Ben asked.

"He didn't break my heart," Africa declared, but her eyes told a different story. The immediate anger that gripped Ben took him by surprise. He was a nonviolent man, but he was glad that this Kwame was not within striking distance.

"Why didn't you tell your mom?" Ben asked. "You used to tell her everything."

"I didn't want to tell Mom, because I didn't want to hear her tell me how she told me that I shouldn't have gotten involved with him from the start. I hate it when she's right and I'm wrong."

"I know that things haven't been so great between the two of you lately, but, honey, this isn't the way to handle things. You don't run away."

Africa looked directly at him. "You do."

Her words hit him in the gut.

Africa went on. "You run away, Dad. You travel all the time."

"It's called 'working for a living,'" Ben defended himself. "Traveling is a part of my job. I'm a journalist. I write about things that happen all over the world."

Africa let out a long sigh. "It's called running, Dad. You choose assignments that take you away. And you travel all over the world, but when was the last time you came to California to see me?"

"Seven months ago," Ben replied. "When I came out to L.A., you hardly had any time for me."

"That's a cop-out, and you know it."

His daughter had him there. He'd been uncomfortable with Africa in L.A. Seeing her in the world that she inhabited, a world that he knew very little about, had hurt him. He had realized how much he'd missed in his daughter's life, and instead of letting that be the impetus to bring them closer, Ben had retreated.

Ben did what any busted parent would do under the circumstances. He changed the subject.

"This is about you, not me," he said. "What you did was wrong. You could have gotten hurt. If you wanted to see me, why didn't you just call me? I would have tried to work something out with your mother. I would have sent you a ticket."

"You guys are still fighting over me. So I took matters into my own hands."

"What if I'd been away on assignment?" Ben asked. "I was in Jamaica when you arrived. What if I hadn't come back for a while?"

"I know where you keep your emergency cash. In the third volume of your *Encyclopædia Britannica*. And I know how to order food deliveries. You have practically every DVD known to man stocked here. I'd be fine."

"That's not the point. What you did was wrong.

It was irresponsible. You've hurt a lot of people. Not just your mother. I'm sure your grandmothers are worried sick."

"I was going to call them," Africa said. "I was going to go to Nana's house in Harlem, but I changed my mind at the last minute and decided to chill here. Plus, I didn't know if Nana would be too happy to see Buddy."

"I take it you're referring to the dog," Ben said.

Africa nodded as she petted Buddy's head.

"Africa, I'm not too happy to see Buddy." Ben kept his voice even, even as the exasperation he felt threatened to push him over the edge. He didn't want to start yelling at her like a raving lunatic, but after the last few days, seeing Buddy the wonder dog in his apartment might just be his undoing, Ben reasoned.

"He's a beagle," Africa said proudly.

"I don't care if he's a Chihuahua mixed with a Siamese cat. I don't want him here."

Buddy started barking, as if he knew that he was being talked about in a less-than-flattering manner.

Tears welled up in Africa's eyes. "He's a rescue dog. He doesn't have anywhere to go. I picked him up a few months ago. Kwame was keeping him for me. You know how Mom feels about animals. . . ."

"The same way I do?"

"Exactly." So, anyway, when Kwame and I broke up, he gave Buddy back to me. I'm all he's got, Dad."

He hated it when his daughter cried. He'd been the kind of parent that parenting books warned him not to be. When his daughter was a baby, he'd pick her up and hold her until the tears ceased.

Even now, these many years later, the sight of her tears was going to win him over. *Dammit*. He could feel his resolve weakening.

"All right, the dog stays for now," said Ben. "But it goes back with you when you go to L.A. I'm not going to baby-sit a dog. I'm not going to do what Kwame did."

Africa flashed him a triumphant grin, and Ben had the suspicion that he'd just been played by his daughter.

"Thanks, Dad! You're the best."

Buddy barked his approval.

Another dog had come into his life. Ben shook his head. Was the Lord trying to tell him something? His life was complicated enough. As Buddy wagged his tail and looked up at him, Ben had a sinking feeling that he was going to be stuck with this dog for a long time.

"Go call your mother," he said to Africa. "Let her know that you'll be with me for the next few days, until we can sort this all out."

Chapter 22

"I'm not going back to New York," Belinda Rose declared to her two daughters. "I'm staying here in Jamaica until the baby's born."

"Mom, be reasonable," Roxie implored. "You hate Jamaica. You hate Aunt Beryl, and you hate Dad."

"She's got a point there," Sinclair chimed in, hoping to save her sister from having to spend the next few months living with their mother.

Belinda Rose pursed her lips. Then, she said, "I don't hate Jamaica."

Since arriving in Jamaica, her mother, whom Sinclair would normally describe as being impossible, had taken her difficult nature to a whole other level. Belinda Rose had openly feuded with Cassius and Beryl over everything from the food that they were giving Roxie (too spicy) to the obstetrician whom Cassius had recommended (too young). In addition, her frequent ominous predictions about the horrors of childbirth in a place that was a far cry from New York City only served to ensure that folks ran in the other direction whenever Belinda Rose was around.

Unfortunately for Sinclair, she couldn't run from her mother. Like her sister, Sinclair had to simply grin and bear it. The one silver lining in the situation, however, was the knowledge that Belinda Rose would soon be leaving for New York. That scenario, however, didn't seem to be happening any time soon.

Sinclair let the afternoon breeze on the veranda, which was fast becoming one of her favorite places, soothe her. She'd spent most of the afternoon on the veranda, drinking lemonade and talking with Roxie. It had been a peaceful and enjoyable afternoon until their mother had descended on them with her less-than-welcome news.

Sinclair tried to talk some sense into her mother. "Mom, Roxie's got everything under control. You don't need to worry about anything. You can come back with me, like we planned."

Belinda Rose was sitting in a pretty pink wooden rocking chair. As her mother vigorously rocked back and forth, Sinclair could see her pursed lips and narrow eyes—sure signs that her mother wasn't going to change her position in this matter.

"I'm not leaving my daughter in her time of need," Belinda Rose said as she fanned herself.

"Mom, please. I'll be fine." Roxie looked panic-stricken.

"Yes, you will." Belinda Rose continued fanning herself and rocking back and forth. "Because I'll be here with you."

At that particular moment, Cassius walked out onto the veranda, with a glass of water. He handed the water to Roxie and said to his pregnant daughter, "Drink up. You need to be hydrated."

Roxie took the water from her father. "Mom's staying with me until the baby's born," she said.

Sinclair waited for the storm of protest that was surely going to erupt from her father. Her father's dislike of her mother had now taken on legendary proportions.

"That sounds like a great idea," her father said mildly as he waited for Roxie to finish drinking her glass of water.

Both Roxie and Sinclair stared, openmouthed, at their father. Even Belinda Rose appeared to be surprised.

"But, Dad, you've got everything under control here," Sinclair said slowly, trying to get her father to understand the full implications of having her mother around during Roxie's pregnancy. She was going to drive everyone crazy, including the one person who needed her wits about her—Roxie.

"That's true, honey," her father replied as he took the empty glass away from Roxie. "However, if your mother wants to be here for Roxie, then I think that's a great idea."

Sinclair watched as her father walked back inside the house. Then, she turned to her mother and asked, "What was that about? Did you and Dad talk about your staying here with Roxie?"

Belinda Rose shook her head. "I don't know what's gotten into him," she said, sounding suspicious and not at all happy to get support from that unlikely ally. "But my decision remains the same. I'm staying here until my new grandbaby is born."

Sinclair looked over at her stricken sister. Shaking

her head, she mouthed the words, "Heaven help you!"

If Cassius could have danced a jig, he would have, but he wanted to hide his elation—there really was no other word for it—over the fact that his aggravating, stubborn, judgmental, beautiful ex-wife was going to be in close proximity for the next few months. He didn't want her to know just how happy this news made him feel. This was the second chance he'd been praying for, the second chance to show her that he would put her and the family first—before his practice, before anything else. He'd messed up before, but he'd never make that mistake again. Taking care of Roxie was going to be his first priority, and wooing her very difficult mother would be his second. Belinda Rose was going to resist, but if she didn't kill him first, maybe he just might have a shot. Despite his best efforts at keeping cool, Cassius could not contain his deep laughter, which rang through the lobby area as he walked back to the kitchen. Things were about to get even more interesting around the inn.

Chapter 23

Princess, the Yorkshire terrier, was not happy. Sinclair had been in Jamaica for almost two weeks, and when she returned to her small apartment, she faced an angry terrier. She knew that Kiki had taken good care of Princess, but it was clear that Princess had missed her, and she was going to make Sinclair pay for being away so long. After her initial greeting, complete with excessive tail wagging and loud barking, Princess had apparently remembered that Sinclair had left her behind to go on a trip, and the dog proceeded to ignore Sinclair for the rest of the day.

After a day of traveling by car, Sinclair had taken the early morning flight out of Montego Bay that was bound for New York. She'd felt terrible leaving Roxie behind, but in the end she knew that Roxie was right. Sinclair had responsibilities in New York that she needed to take care of. She'd assuaged her guilt at leaving her sister by making plans to come back to spend the last month of Roxie's pregnancy with her in Jamaica. She wanted to be there when her sister went into labor.

It was good to be home, even if home was a cramped New York City apartment with an angry dog. She looked over at Princess, who was lying on a pink and white, heart-shaped dog bed. Princess was staring at Sinclair, but she made no move to come any closer.

Sinclair took out a treat and held it in Princess's direction. "Come here, baby," she said to her recalcitrant dog.

Princess turned her head in another direction and completely ignored Sinclair.

"I'll make it up to you," Sinclair promised her canine companion. Princess got up from her dog bed and walked out of the living room area and into the kitchen. All attempts at reconciliation were apparently being ignored. With the exception of Princess's occasional low-pitched growl, the apartment was eerily quiet.

Sinclair turned her attention to the telephone. She thought about calling Ben, but she wasn't sure what to say. They hadn't spoken to each other in over a week, and during that time, she'd started having second thoughts about him. She wasn't sure if she was ready for a relationship, and that seemed to be what Ben was interested in. She was equally uninterested in just being a conquest. She didn't know what she wanted from Ben. As a result, Sinclair decided to let things simmer until she made a decision. Maybe she'd call him in a few weeks.

There was, however, someone else she needed to speak to. Picking up the receiver, she dialed

Everett's telephone number. She'd been thinking about him a lot over the past few days, and she wanted to reach out to him and to see how he was doing. She'd never understood how, after breakups, families that were once close became virtual strangers. It was one thing if the breakup came as a result of violent acts or continued wrongdoing, but Everett was the wounded party. Sinclair didn't see any benefit in ignoring her brother-in-law. She'd liked him when he was with Roxie, and now that they were apart, she wasn't going to stop liking him.

After the first ring, Everett's answering machine switched on, inviting the caller to leave a message. "Hi. It's me. Sinclair." She hated to just leave a message on the machine, but she suspected that for the time being, Everett was probably going to screen all calls. Although it was past seven o'clock in the evening, there was the possibility that Everett was at work, but she doubted that he was working this late. "I'm back in New York. I just called to tell you that if you need anything, anything at all, please give me a call. No matter what happened between you and Roxie, I still care for you. Everett, I hope you're okay. Bye."

Sinclair placed the telephone back in the cradle; then she stretched out on the couch. Intending to take a short nap, she fell into a deep sleep.

Two weeks of living with a teenager had almost driven Ben to drink. He loved his daughter dearly, but there were times that he had to remind himself of that basic fact. The last time Africa had come to visit him, she'd been reasonable, fun, and

good company. That was then; this was now. He'd
seen a change in her when he'd gone to California
to see her for a few days, and it hadn't been a
change for the better. She'd been more interested
in hanging out with her friends than with her
father. Ben couldn't blame her for that. It had
been months since they'd seen each other, and
their stilted weekly telephone calls didn't make
things any better. But as difficult as the visit to California had been, this was worse—infinitely worse.

All Africa wanted to do was to lie around the
apartment and watch rap videos. The only thing
that got her out of her stupor was the dog, who had
already ruined two pairs of his shoes—the most expensive ones. Buddy had peed on one pair, and the
other pair had been used as some sort of teething
ring. The dog was not toilet trained, despite
Africa's declaration to the contrary, and Ben had
found some unpleasant surprises around the apartment. It was now almost ten o'clock in the evening,
and Africa was watching a reality show about a for-
merly famous rap star who was choosing the new
stripper for his video—hardly educational or responsible television. But Ben and Africa had been
fighting all day, and the relative peace that the
show afforded him was welcome. He knew he
wouldn't win any Father of the Year awards with
this particular parental choice. But what else could
he do? His daughter was already on birth control.
A stripper in a video wasn't going to corrupt her
any more than she had, apparently, already been
corrupted.

Buddy was locked up in a crate, and he was barking. Ben was sure that the demon dog wanted to

roam free so he could urinate with impunity on some other expensive piece of clothing or nibble on some furniture. Ben was trying the crate method of housebreaking the dog. He'd read that the proper way to potty train a dog was to put the dog in a small cage, called a crate, where it apparently would not relieve itself, and to take it out periodically so it understood that the place to go to the bathroom was outside the home, and not anywhere it felt like going. The training had gone well the first few days, until Africa decided that this tried and true method was downright cruel. Every chance she got, she would sneak Buddy out of the crate, and he would inevitably roam free and relieve himself.

He'd spoken to Leneta about Africa, and she'd told him that she would be coming to New York to get her daughter. That was a week ago. Every day he asked her when she was coming for Africa, and she'd tell him that she was working on it. He'd offered to send her an airline ticket, but Leneta had refused. "I can afford a ticket," she'd huffed, but she still hadn't made any definite plans. Now that she knew her daughter was safe, she was in no hurry to come and get her.

This had been what Ben had hoped for, an extended period of time with his daughter, but that was before she became a veritable agent of the devil. He tried to be understanding. His daughter had been through a lot—starting with shuttling between two warring parents. He also knew that he hadn't been the stabilizing presence in her life that she'd needed. Then, there was this whole broken heart thing. He didn't know how to help her on

that one. In his mind, if this guy Kwame didn't
want her, he was either blind or stupid or both. His
daughter was beautiful and smart. She'd find another boyfriend, although he was hoping that she
wouldn't find another boyfriend until she finished
college and graduate school and was gainfully em-
ployed. Boys were trouble. He ought to know; he'd
been a boy once.

He couldn't understand Africa mooning over
anyone. She was much too practical, much too self-
involved. But here she was, eating popcorn, watching MTV, and staring moodily at her father
whenever Ben tried to strike up a conversation with
her. He'd sought advice from his mother, who had
responded unhelpfully that he had been a difficult
child himself, and perhaps this was just a little bit of
payback. Leneta's mother had urged the use of
prayer and the belt. Ben believed in prayer, but at
this point he was willing to take things one step further. He wanted to take his child to the exorcist to
cast out whatever demons were now inhabiting her
soul. As for the belt, he couldn't bring himself to ad-
minister corporal punishment. The exorcist was
looking like his best option.

The telephone rang, and Buddy started howling.
This was yet another annoying trait the undisci-
plined beagle exhibited. He would howl periodically, a sound that grated on Ben's nerves. Buddy
loved howling in the middle of the night—a
mournful, soul-cringing sound that neither Ben
nor his neighbors appreciated, judging from the
anonymous poison pen note slipped under his
door this morning. The dog was going to get him
evicted.

"Hello," Ben growled into the telephone.

"Hey, buddy." It was Everett. Ben's spirits rose instantly. He hadn't talked to his friend since they'd come back from Jamaica. Ben had left him several messages, but none of his calls were returned.

"Don't call me that," Ben replied, thinking of the pestering dog. "How are you?"

"I've been better. What's going on? Sounds like I caught you at a bad time."

Ben let out a deep sigh. "Africa's visiting," he said.

"That's great, man! I didn't know she was coming to New York!"

"Neither did I," Ben said wearily. "She ran away from home, and she brought a dog."

"Ouch."

"The dog's name is Buddy."

"Say no more, my friend. Your hatred of animals is well documented."

"I don't hate them." Ben suddenly felt defensive. Buddy had stopped howling, and he was now staring at him. When he was quiet, Buddy was actually cute. Oh hell! What was happening to him? He was actually starting to develop some feelings for this four-legged creature who'd turned his life upside down. "I just don't want to live with them. I'm perfectly happy for pets to live with someone else, just not in my house."

"Looks like you have your hands full."

"I'd say that and then some. What's going on? You sound like you're feeling better," said Ben.

"Not really," Everett replied. "But I haven't jumped in front of a moving truck yet, so I think I'm making progress."

"Have you heard from her?" Ben asked, refer-ring to Roxie.

"No, but I heard from Sinclair. She's back in town."

Ben couldn't swear to it, but he thought he could hear angels singing the Hallelujah chorus in the distance.

"When did she get back?" Ben asked.

"Not sure. She left a message. That's why I'm calling. You need to call her."

Ben was touched. Although his friend was going through hell, he still picked up the telephone to bring him what Everett must have known was wel-come news. They hadn't had a chance to talk about Sinclair, but Ben was certain that his feelings for her were obvious.

"I'll call her," Ben said. "Look, Everett, let's get together."

"I'll get back to you," Everett replied. "I'm not the best company right now."

"Do you think I give a damn about that?" Ben asked. "I just want to be there for a good friend."

"You've already been there for me. You've got nothing to prove. Right now, your hands are full. Sounds like Africa and the dog are giving you a run for the money. I think Sinclair might just be what the doctor ordered."

He doesn't know the half of it, Ben said to himself as a vision of Sinclair lying in his arms flashed through his mind.

"She's a good woman," Everett said, "but you already know that."

"Yes," said Ben. "I do."

"So what are you waiting on? Get off the phone with me, and go give her a call."

Ben hung up the telephone after talking a little while longer with Everett. He wanted to call Sinclair, but it was now after ten o'clock at night. He knew that hearing her voice wouldn't be enough. He needed to see her, but he couldn't leave Africa in the apartment this late. As much as he wanted to lose himself in Sinclair Dearheart's arms, he had a responsibility to his daughter, and spending the night with a woman while his daughter stayed at home, unattended, wasn't the kind of father he wanted to be. He knew that if he went over to her apartment, he wasn't leaving until morning. Their attraction to each other was undeniable, and he had very persuasive ways when it came to breaking down Sinclair's reserve. Besides, if she knew that he'd left his daughter to make love with her, he wouldn't hear the last of it. He hadn't known Sinclair that long, but he'd known her long enough to know that she wasn't that kind of woman, and it only made him more attracted to her. Suppressing a sigh, he turned his attention back to the book on housebreaking dogs. He'd have to call Sinclair tomorrow.

There had to be about a million stars in the ink black sky. Belinda Rose hated to admit it, but Jamaica was a beautiful place. As she sat in the garden at Beryl's inn, she looked up at the sky and the outline of the mountains. She'd gotten used to the heat, and even though it was still warm at night, it was no longer uncomfortable. She'd spent the past few weeks trying to make peace with her daughter. She knew that Roxie hadn't wanted her to stay, and she'd been hurt by that. She also knew that she was largely to blame for her daughter's reluctance to have her around. She hadn't made things easy for either of her daughters. Belinda Rose's mother had raised her to be a tough woman. She hadn't gotten many hugs and kisses from her own mother: she'd thought that hugs and kisses would make Belinda Rose soft. However, Belinda Rose's mother had been completely different with both of her granddaughters and had spoiled them rotten.

Belinda Rose believed in hugs and kisses, but she also believed in tough love. She knew that both of her daughters shared Cassius's soft heart, and she'd worried about them. She'd tried to toughen them up to prepare them for what lay ahead for them, but they'd still experienced heartbreak. Hell, as tough as she was, she'd had her heart broken, too.

"Can I join you?" Cassius's deep voice interrupted her reverie.

She was tempted to tell him to go away. She'd tried to avoid him, but over the last few days, everywhere she'd turned, he'd been there—with that patient, waiting expression. The ruder she treated him, the nicer he got. He refused to take offense at anything she said. She'd even overheard him defending her to his sister Beryl, who'd described her as a "virago" and an "interfering shrew."

"It's a free country," Belinda Rose responded.

Cassius sat beside her. They were silent for a moment. Then, Cassius said softly, "I've always hoped you'd come to spend time in my country."

Belinda Rose chuckled. "I avoided it as long as I could," she said. "It took Roxie's . . . er . . . predicament to get me here."

"And now that you're here, what do you think of our little island?"

Belinda Rose looked up at the star-filled sky and listened to the sounds of the crickets and night insects. It was oddly comforting.

"I think your little island is just beautiful," Belinda Rose admitted. "I can see why you love it here."

"Why didn't you come with me to visit when we were married?" Cassius asked. "You always refused."

Belinda Rose thought about the question for a few moments before she answered. "I think I was jealous," she admitted. "I thought you loved this place more than you loved me."

"I have never loved any person, place, or thing more than I have loved you, Belle."

Cassius Dearheart had been the only man who had loved her even after knowing her worst faults. He had accepted her—warts and all. He'd never tried to change her—even when she was at her most outrageous. When they were dating, she'd tried her best to scare him away by acting as obnoxious, unpredictable, and downright rude to him as possible. But he'd only held on tighter, when he should have let her go. In the end, she'd let him go, because she was jealous of his passion for his career. She'd been jealous of anything that took his attention from her, including Jamaica. She'd been a fool. She could see that now. She'd walked away from a good man—a good man who had faults, but a good man, nonetheless.

She didn't trust herself to speak. She felt like throwing herself into his arms and sobbing her heart out, but she had too much pride for that. Instead, she sat up straighter and concentrated on the stars.

She felt his hand take hers, and it was almost her undoing.

"Belle, I made so many mistakes," Cassius said. "If I could do it all over again, I'd do things so differently. I know that's the refrain of many a foolish husband, but I honestly mean it. As much as my practice meant to me, you and the girls meant more."

"Why didn't you show us that we meant more?" Belinda Rose asked, her voice cracking.

Cassius shook his head. "I thought I did, Belle. I'm sorry."

In spite of all her rigorous home training to be a stoical, strong, take-no-prisoners woman, she felt a teardrop roll down her face. She was mortified. She knew that Cassius could see that she was crying.

Cassius raised her hand to his lips and kissed it softly. "I've been a fool," he said.

Belle wiped her tears with her free hand. "An old fool," she said. "We've both been old fools."

Cassius kissed her hand again. "Do you think it's too late for two old fools to change their ways?" he asked.

Belle gave her ex-husband a sly smile. "I don't know, Cassius. But I'm willing to try. Are you?"

The next morning, Ben woke up and cooked breakfast. He didn't order it from the deli, as he'd been doing ever since he'd moved into the apartment. He'd gone shopping the night before, and he cooked oatmeal, eggs, and turkey bacon for his daughter. He also squeezed oranges and made fresh orange juice. His hands were cramped, but it was worth the effort. He had to admit that his orange juice gave the store-bought orange juice a run for its money.

He had awakened with a new sense of purpose. After having a long talk with Africa's mother last night, they'd decided to let Africa stay with him for a while. It was clear Africa needed something different, and it was also clear that Ben needed to step up his game as a father. This was what he'd prayed for—the chance to spend some real time being a father to his daughter. God had answered his prayers in the affirmative, and just because his daughter had turned into a rebellious teenager didn't mean they didn't have a chance to finally get to know each other. He was going to take that chance.

He placed the breakfast on a tray and carried it into the guest bedroom, where Africa was sleeping. She woke up as he entered the room.

"What's this?" she asked, sitting up.

"Some call it breakfast," Ben said, placing the tray on her bed. "I call it a truce."

"Did someone cook this?" Africa asked, confused.

"It smells like someone actually used the kitchen. Did you hire a cook?"

Ben picked up a piece of turkey bacon and began eating. *Not bad,* he thought as he sampled his handiwork. "I made breakfast."

"You cooked?" Africa squealed.

Ben nodded his head.

"What's going on?"

"I'm glad you asked. It looks like you'll be staying here for a while."

"You're not kicking me out?" Africa asked. "Yesterday you referred to me as a demon child."

"True enough. But you're my demon child, and your mom thinks it's a good idea if you stay with me for a while."

"How long is a while?"

"I don't know," Ben replied honestly. "Let's just see how this works one day at a time, and all that."

"Are you going to hassle me like Mom?"

"I'm a parent. Hassling my kid is part of my DNA. Speaking of which, we need to go over the ground rules. No watching television the whole day. I want you to find something to do. I was thinking you like animals, and I have a friend who owns a pet clinic. Maybe you could volunteer to help out."

"A friend?" Africa asked as she dug into her oatmeal with gusto. "What kind of friend? A woman friend?"

"Yeah." Ben grinned as he ate his second slice of turkey bacon. "Her name is Sinclair. I'm hoping to convince her to be my girlfriend."

"Well, you're not that bad looking," Africa said thoughtfully. "Although you probably have to work a little bit on your personality. I can help you, Dad."

"Thanks, but no thanks." Ben laughed at his daughter. She actually thought of him as a project.

"Dad, your wardrobe is lame. Maybe we can go shopping, and I can hook you up with some new outfits."

"Fair enough," Ben agreed. Then, he asked, "You don't mind that I may have a woman in my life?"

"Is she an empty-headed bimbo?"

Ben laughed aloud. When he finally stopped laughing, he responded, "No. Her name is Sinclair, and she's not an empty-headed bimbo."

"Then I don't mind. It's about time."

"Okay, let's go back to the ground rules. No sex. You're too young."

"Dad!" Africa was clearly embarrassed. "The birth-control pills were a precautionary move. We never did it."

"Well, whether you did or you didn't, you won't be doing it here."

"Any other ground rules?"

"Put away your clothes after you wear them, pick up after yourself, and start reading a book. I don't care what the book is, but it's time to do something other than watch television."

"You'd be a good prison warden, Dad."

"Thanks," Ben replied. "I'll take that as a compliment. Hurry up and finish eating. We're going furniture shopping. We need to get you some new furniture for your room."

"This is going to be my room?"

"For as long as you want it."

"So I get to decorate it the way I want to?"

"Yes," Ben replied. "As long as you don't put any pictures of naked men on the wall."

"Dad!" Africa squealed again, but Ben could see the laughter in his daughter's eyes. He gave a silent prayer of thanks.

Chapter 24

"This is Sinclair, the Pet Diva. I'm back and ready to talk with you about your pets. Tell me, what's going on with the pets in your life?"

Sinclair settled in and started discussing topics ranging from pet separation anxiety to when to let a terminal pet die in peace and dignity. It felt good to be back doing what she knew best—talking about animals.

"Next caller," she purred into the microphone, getting back into the groove. She'd missed doing this.

"Is this the Pet Diva?" a masculine, very sexy, and, by now, very familiar voice asked over the radio telephone. It couldn't be. How did he know she was back?

Sinclair felt her heart hammering in her chest.

Taking a deep breath, she said, "Yes, it is, sir. What can I do for you?"

She heard a deep chuckle over the line, and she knew for certain that the caller was none other than Ben Easington.

"Well, now that's an open-ended question . . . I'm sure I can think of many things that you can do for me," said Ben.

Her assistant, Melody, raised a puzzled eyebrow.

Sinclair cleared her throat. "Is there any question that you have about a pet, sir?"

She heard another chuckle. "As a matter of fact, I do have a question about a pet," replied Ben.

Sinclair was flustered. Since when did Ben care about anything to do with pets? "You do? I thought you hated animals."

"I don't hate animals," Ben replied. "In fact, I've just acquired a beagle."

Melody scribbled some words on a piece of paper and held it up for Sinclair to read: WHO IS THIS GUY, AND DO YOU KNOW HIM?

Sinclair nodded her head.

"What's going on with your beagle?" Sinclair asked, clearing her throat.

"He pees all over my house, chews my furniture and shoes, and howls through the night."

"Sounds like you're not giving him enough attention," Sinclair replied, her heart still hammering. It was positively sinful what this man's voice did to her. If she'd thought that her attraction to Ben had waned over the last few weeks, she'd been wrong. Dead wrong.

"That's what I think, but I can't be sure," Ben replied. "I was hoping you'd make a house call."

"Out of the question," said Sinclair.

"Please?" Ben asked. "I'd make it worth your while. . . ."

This had gone on long enough. She motioned to Mike to go to a commercial break. During the commercial break, she took the phone off speaker and started talking to Ben.

"You're a maniac," she said, but she couldn't contain her laughter.

"What time do you get off work?" he asked. "I want to see you."

"I'll be off the air in an hour."

"Good," Ben replied. "I'll pick you up."

"You don't know where I work."

"Yes, I do. And Sinclair?"

"Yes, Ben?"

"I've missed you."

Sinclair was still smiling when she hung up the telephone.

It was three o'clock in the afternoon, and Everett hadn't gotten out of bed. He'd been awake for hours, but other than channel surfing through daytime television shows, he hadn't done much of anything. This was his routine. His sister called it depression. He called it getting his heart ripped out by the woman he loved. It didn't matter what anyone called it, he was hurting, and he was hurting badly. He'd taken a leave of absence from his job, but he knew that he was going to have to go back soon, or he'd end up getting fired. He knew that he had to pull himself together, but for the life of him, he just couldn't do it.

He heard someone banging on his front door.

"Go away!" he yelled.

The banging continued.

"I said, go away!" Everett yelled louder.

The banging on the door continued until

Everett got up. Walking over to the door, he pulled it open, determined to curse out whoever it was that was using his door as a drum.

He found himself facing a very worried-looking Cassius.

"May I come in?" Cassius asked.

"Actually, I'm busy right now," Everett replied.

Cassius took in the rumpled T-shirt and plaid pajama pants. "I can see that," he said as he pushed past Everett and walked into Everett's apartment.

"This really isn't a good time," Everett said.

"On the contrary," Cassius said as he walked over to a chair and sat down. "This is the perfect time."

"I don't feel like talking right now," Everett said to his father-in-law. "I just want to be left alone."

"Sit down," Cassius commanded, and damned if Everett didn't obey the old man. He sat down on one of the arms of his sofa. The sofa and every other piece of furniture in the apartment had been chosen by Roxie. That thought brought a fresh stab of pain.

"I know what it's like to want to be left alone," Cassius continued. "I felt the same way when Belinda Rose asked me to leave. All I wanted to do was be left alone, and for the past twenty years, I've gotten my wish. Guess what? It turns out that being left alone wasn't the best thing for me. It isn't the best thing for you, either, son."

Everett snorted. "I don't mean to be rude, but your daughter cheated on me! She's carrying another man's baby!"

Cassius nodded his head. "She did cheat on you,

and she could be carrying another man's baby. She also ran away from you. I can't justify her actions."

"Then why the hell are you here?" Everett asked.

"I'm here because I don't want you to make the same mistake I did."

"Which was?"

"I walked out on the woman I loved because my pride was hurt."

Everett snorted again. "I think this is a little bit more serious than hurt pride."

"I'll give you that," Cassius said. "You have every right to sit here and feel sorry for yourself, but is this how you want to live your life?"

"Your daughter didn't give me much choice."

"This really isn't about Roxie," said Cassius. "She didn't put a gun to your head and demand that you lock yourself up in your apartment while life passes you by."

"She might as well have," Everett snarled. "If you don't mind, I've grown tired of this conversation. I appreciate you coming by, but I'd like you to leave."

Cassius stood up. "Fair enough. But the baby she's carrying could be yours. If a woman was carrying my baby, I'd make it my business to be there with her, even if it was only to make sure that my baby would know me."

"We don't know if it's my baby."

"We don't know that it isn't."

Everett's pride stung. Who was this man to come here and challenge the way he was living? It was his daughter that had caused this whole mess. "You're a hypocrite, Cassius. You walked away from two children."

"And I'll regret that until the day I die." Cassius replied. "Do you want to make the same mistake I did? I should have fought for my family, and even if Belinda Rose went through with the divorce, I shouldn't have left my girls because I couldn't bear being around their mother. It was wrong. It was cowardly, and I'd give my right arm and my left to do things over again, but I can't. I can't bring back those years I lost with my girls. Only the biggest kind of fool would follow in my footsteps. You need to be with your wife. Even if you don't love her anymore, that child could be yours. You should be there to make sure your child comes into this world knowing you."

"What if it isn't my child?" Everett asked, his voice hollow.

"Then you would have done a fatherless child a good deed. You told Roxie that you'd be there if the child turns out to be yours."

"That's true."

"And if it turns out to be yours, and you miss the next five months of your child's existence, would it be worth it? Phillip doesn't want anything to do with the child even if it is his."

"Well, that's the man your daughter chose."

"That's the man she slept with, and she regrets that more than she could ever possibly say. She chose you. She did a terrible thing, and only you can decide if you want to forgive her. I can't tell you to do that. I'm not sure I could do that if I were in your shoes, and Roxie is my daughter. But don't turn your back on your baby. Roxie very well might be carrying your baby. You should be there to help her through this. But, hell, it's up to you. I've said all I have to say. I have a plane to catch in two hours."

The time it took Ben to walk through the front door of her apartment and end up in her bed made Sinclair blush with shame. She had truly become a wild woman, and she didn't care. She'd tried to tell herself to take it slow. She tried to tell herself that maybe it wasn't time to get serious. Considering her disastrous last relationship, Sinclair didn't trust her judgment. But one look at Ben convinced her that maybe, just maybe, her heart had finally found a home.

They made love again and again. Even Princess was impressed. She'd broken her stance on exile, and she'd come into the bedroom with Ben and Sinclair. After their last bout of lovemaking, Sinclair had lain in Ben's arms, exhausted and happy.

"I have something to tell you," he said.

"Mmmm." Sinclair shifted in his arms to get more comfortable. She thought dreamily that she could lie happily with Ben forever. "What is it?"

"My daughter might be moving in with me."

"Ben, that's great!" Sinclair was genuinely happy for him. She knew how hard it had been when his daughter had moved away to California.

Ben sighed. "You haven't met her. Trust me, you'll have a far different opinion when you meet her. I've been trying to get her mother to come take her home, but she finally admitted today that she needed a break. Actually, that they both needed a break from each other. Africa is going to spend some time with me, and maybe if it works out, she'll enroll in school in New York. Her mom thinks maybe a change of scenery would be a good thing."

"What about your traveling?" Sinclair asked. She'd heard about his extensive globe-trotting from Everett and from Roxie.

"Her grandmothers are both in New York. They've offered to help, and I've already told the magazine that I need to cut back. They've been supportive."

Sinclair snuggled in his arms. "They don't want to lose their star reporter."

"How about you?" Ben asked. "Do you want to lose this star reporter?"

Sinclair didn't answer immediately. She didn't know what to say. When he'd asked her to be with him in Jamaica, she'd gotten scared. She knew that they were attracted to each other, and although it had only been a short time since they'd met, she knew they cared for each other. But she also knew that once she gave her heart to Ben, really gave her heart, not just her body, there would be no turning back.

Was she ready for this? It had taken a while to get her life back after Wayne left. Her life was now in order. There was no drama. But there was something missing, something she hadn't known was missing until Ben had walked out on the patio and surprised her at Roxie's wedding rehearsal dinner. She didn't believe in love at first sight, but there was something about Ben Easington that, even from the start, she'd known was different from other men she'd been with. This was a man who was not going to let her sit on the sidelines, watching life go by. This was a man who was going to grab her and thrust her full throttle into the ride of her life. Was she ready for this?

Sinclair looked up into his eyes and saw love. In that one moment, she decided to take a chance. She had a lot to lose if it didn't work out, but she was beginning to come to the conclusion that a safe, orderly life just might be overrated. She needed more, and a life with Ben might just be what the doctor ordered. Maybe it was time to shake things up. Maybe it was time to get things complicated. Doing what was expected of her hadn't prevented her from experiencing heartache. She'd been a good wife, a good person. She'd eaten her vegetables, exercised every day, cooked wonderful meals, listened attentively to Wayne's needs, and she'd lived right. Wayne had still walked out on her. Sometimes life wasn't fair, but sometimes life gave second chances. What the hell, Sinclair thought, as she stared into Ben's eyes, she had a lot to lose, namely her heart, but she had a lot to gain also. She had second chance.

"Do you want to lose this star reporter?" Ben asked again.

In that one defining moment, she decided to take the leap of faith. She decided to follow her heart.

"Heavens, no!" Sinclair declared as the star reporter in question started nuzzling her neck.

"Don't you ever get tired?" Sinclair teased as she realized that the lovemaking was about to continue.

Ben pulled her closer. After giving her a light bite on her neck, one of her most sensitive areas, he drawled, "Actually, no. It's part of my charm."

"What about your daughter?" Sinclair asked.

"She's with her grandmother. We've got all night."

Epilogue

The birth of Faith Belinda Rose Dunn was a family affair. Faith's mother had gone into labor two days before the birth, which had given the family members who'd traveled from New York City enough time to get to the island of Jamaica and to make the trek to the small hospital in Port Antonio before her actual appearance. It had not been an easy birth, and Faith had come into the world screaming. But her parents, Roxie and Everett, had been beside themselves with pride, happiness, and relief that their little girl had finally shown up and, despite dire predictions from her maternal grandmother, was healthy, with all the requisite body parts intact.

Sinclair had cried when she first saw her niece. She was beautiful and she was perfect. She looked exactly like Roxie, except she had the same widow's peak and deep dimples as Everett. It wouldn't have mattered if Faith had come out looking like someone else. Everett had made up his mind a long time ago that he loved his wife, and he had forgiven her. His love for the baby Roxie was carrying was equally unconditional. It had taken his father-in-law to talk some sense into him. He'd resigned his job and flown to Jamaica to be with Roxie about a week after Cassius had shown up at his apartment. It had taken a while for Everett and Roxie to work things out, and there were some hurts that he knew would never completely heal. But Everett knew that he loved this woman, and Roxie knew that she loved this man. She also knew that she would never, ever test her love for him, or his love for her. Everett now worked with Aunt Beryl, as the manager at her inn, and there was talk of her aunt expanding and buying another inn. To Sinclair, Everett seemed happy. She'd never really thought he was happy with the New York rat race. Everett and Roxie had decided to raise their family in Jamaica. Roxie was going to start an interior decorating business on the island, and Everett was going to also be her business partner.

The most surprising thing about Faith's arrival was that it had brought the warring maternal grandmother and grandfather together. Although Roxie had informed Sinclair months ago that their parents had reunited, Sinclair still had to see it to believe it. Even when she caught her parents kissing in the garden shortly after they brought little Faith back to Aunt Beryl's inn, she couldn't quite believe her eyes. Who would have thought that after years of warfare, these two legendary combatants would have found their way back to each other? They hadn't decided if they would live in Jamaica or New York, but they knew that wherever they lived, they would be together.

As for Sinclair, she'd inherited a fiancé, a new dog, and a teenager who shared her love of rap music. It wasn't all peaches and cream. There were disagreements with Africa, with trying to juggle a soon-to-be blended family, and Sinclair still had to work on her trust issues. On the plus side, she had a man who was in it for the long haul—or, as he assured her, for better or for worse. Princess, the temperamental Yorkie, loved Africa, but she was still warming up to Ben. As for Buddy, Princess ignored him. Despite Princess's misgivings, as Sinclair held her little niece, Faith, in her arms and watched her fiancé and his daughter swim in her aunt's pool, she felt a feeling of contentment she'd never had in any previous relationship. She felt safe and warm and yes, happy. She knew that there were no perfect storybook endings in real life—but she also knew that she had a chance, a second chance, at finding real love and she was grateful. The Pet Diva had finally found love.

More of the Hottest
African-American Fiction from
Dafina Books